In Search of
Jimmy Buffett

A
KEY WEST
REVIVAL

ASHLEY OLIPHANT

Copyright © 2018 by Ashley Oliphant

ISBN: 978-1-943258-91-8

Oliphant. Ashley.
In Search of Jimmy Buffett: A Key West Revival

Edited by: Allie Coker

Warren publishing

Published by Warren Publishing

Charlotte, NC
www.warrenpublishing.net
Printed in the United States

To the long line of ambitious and fearless Harrill women who have come before me and, most importantly, my mother, Beth. You all awakened and nurtured my creative spirit. As a result, I'm now a novelist.

To my brother, Troy, for loaning me that first Jimmy Buffett album in 1991. Without You Had to Be There *coursing through my consciousness at the age of fourteen, I wouldn't have realized this story before the age of forty.*

And to Jimmy Buffett, for teaching me about the well-crafted story and for exposing the song lines that weave us all together. Your work is a blueprint for the journey, and I'm grateful for it every day. In my better daydreams, the moment will come when I share a pair of barstools and a long conversation with you. I'm buying the first round.

"Shells sink, dreams float
Life's good on our boat."

JIMMY BUFFETT, "DELANEY TALKS TO STATUES"

AUTHOR'S PREFACE

*"Once you've ruined your reputation,
you can live quite freely."*
—RUDYARD KIPLING

The call to write fiction can tailgate your bumper for a long time while you motor down life's highway completely unaware. On a rapturously sunny Key West day in September 2016, I stepped out of Captain Tony's Saloon on Greene Street after an extended sit-down at the bar. I needed non-alcoholic sustenance in the worst way, and Amigo's Tortilla Bar was right across the street with its neon promises of burritos, tacos, enchiladas, and other especiales. Before placing my order, I was drawn to the enormous font of the Rudyard Kipling quote from 1935 that graced the cover of the menu: "Once you've ruined your reputation, you can live quite freely." While I waited for my nachos, I thought about how much fun it would be to fully invest in living by Kipling's mantra. My imagination—already on overload from Key West's barrage of creative stimuli—ran boldly amok, and in that moment, a novel was born.

It mattered not that this was my first creative piece, that I identified only as a nonfiction writer, or that I had a boatload of other things on my desk begging for my attention after this little slice of vacation fizzled. Livie Green waited until I was good and relaxed to lead a conga line through my life, and she refused to leave me be until I told her story. Something that had been covertly marinating in my very own brain got itself ready and began bubbling to the surface of my awareness in wild and unexpected spurts. Images and scenes came into focus with clarity and intensity. There was nothing to be done except stop what I was doing and write them down. The story never left me even as I got on with the business of life and graded papers, waited in line to pick up my son at school, attended committee meetings, and taught college literature classes. It's certainly a bizarre day when you begin to hear the dialogue of your characters for the first time. You wonder whether you should seek medical help for the voices in your head or get a literary agent. I had no choice but to entertain the narrative that began to play through all of my waking moments—and some of my dreams. I'm certainly glad I recognized the earlier incoherent fragments of the emerging story and diligently captured them in my journal.

For the first few months, I had no idea why Livie's story needed to come into print, but I kept writing because the path to her revival made me laugh every single day. Through this book I've learned that fiction is one of the Creator's greatest gifts. Nothing will ever match the feeling of waking up and knowing you get to spend the whole day hanging out in your storyline and seeing what happens to your characters. Once the end product was in sight, I understood that my whole life had been about laying down narrative layers, and, even as a child, I was soaking in events, scenes, characters, details, and dialogue like a very absorbent sponge. What Livie gave me in return was a manifesto for living. While I had never considered the need for such a document, it turns out that we all really must have one.

In 1934, Ernest Hemingway wrote to F. Scott Fitzgerald, insisting, "You ought to write, invent, out of what you know," (*Hemingway Selected Letters, 407*). As I sit wrapping up my fourth book, I find myself in complete agreement with this philosophy. Livie's story is peppered with scenarios and characters from my travels and from my formative years growing up in the Piedmont of North Carolina, an area of the country rich in culinary, linguistic, historical, and cultural heritage. In the middle and late stages of the creation of this story—once I felt more in control of what was happening artistically—the decisions I found myself making about setting, context, dialogue, and character development revealed how central my home was in shaping nearly everything I think, say, and do. If asked, any Southerner can offer stories of ridicule (either by visitors to the South or by the residents of other states) leveled simply because of the place where the speaker was raised: The sidelong glances that inevitably appear when the full extent of one's particular accent or regional turns of phrase are exposed, the jokes about Southerners choking on chicken bones at NASCAR races, the dismissal of the Southern church as a gathering place for the blindly faithful desperate to trust a silly old-time religion. This novel is a celebration of all the distinctive features that have fostered and intensified my love of the South, especially the incredible diversity in its lexicon and pronunciation.

I remember the day in my graduate linguistics course when my beloved professor explained the concept of *language variety*—how every regional version of English represents its own interpretation of the language presented on the page in grammar books. "There is no accent-less language," she said, despite what the broadcasting schools want you to believe. What an empowering moment it was to realize that my Lincoln County, North Carolina version of English was just as valid as that of the haughty Manhattanite who once openly laughed in my face about how ridiculous my accent sounded as I ordered a sandwich in his deli when I was a teenager. I hope this novel will adequately capture my deep respect for Southern speakers—for their creativity, their spunk, and their determination to preserve their traditions in spite of the detractors who simply weren't lucky enough to grow up down here. Just as much, I want this text to convey the extent of my love affair with Key West, the first island that turned my tropical fantasies into a Technicolor reality. I was forever changed the day I drove down the Overseas Highway for the first time, and I've never stopped thinking about it since then.

The readers of this volume who know me well are naturally going to look to the text for connections to real people from my life. The eccentric and fabulous modern poet Marianne Moore famously characterized verse (in a poem called "Poetry," ironically) as the birthing of "imaginary gardens with real toads in them." The garden of this novel is populated by both real and fabricated toads. The Spottswood-Maloney lineage actually exists, and all of the history related to the family I present here is real, but for the character of Luke. Likewise, the connection between the Spottswood family and Mel Fisher is solely a product of my overactive imagination.

Most of the events that are set at Hemingway's Key West house are also not true. The staff members there are a stellar group of professionals who don't, to my knowledge, have nighttime parties on the grounds. Spending a full day there in May 2017 while autographing copies of my last book and simultaneously writing this one simply caused my mind to run wild. I'm the irresponsible one for thinking up such things. As for the genesis of my other characters, I'll bet my house that one of the first questions will relate to the origin of Mama Green. It is important to clarify here that Mama Green has absolutely no correlation to my real mama, Beth Yarbrough of Lincolnton, NC, who is a lovely woman not afflicted with any of the -isms or idiosyncrasies observed in the story. She's delightful—really—and I have not been paid, tortured, or threatened in any way to publish this statement. The narrow thread that separates fact and fiction is easily traversed, but I promise I haven't crossed that threshold with the neurotic matriarch of this book.

Finally, my preface must acknowledge the presence of Jimmy Buffett, both in the story and in my everyday existence. He is the writer of the soundtrack of my life, the singer whose songs initiated the Key West itch in my spirit long before I had the privilege of witnessing its grandeur in person. I was schooled in the proper construction of an island caper by underappreciated works like, *Where is Joe Merchant?*, *Tales from Margaritaville*, and *A Salty Piece of Land*. After you have studied the great writers, there is no way to compose without all of them looking over your shoulder, the residue of their brilliant sentences shaping your own thoughts as they prepare to hit the page. T.S. Eliot wrote in "Tradition and the Individual Talent" that "No poet, no artist of any art, has his complete meaning alone. His significance, his appreciation is the appreciation of his relation to the dead poets and artists. You cannot value him alone; you must set him, for contrast and comparison, among the dead," (1093).

If Mr. Buffett ever has an opportunity to read this book, I hope he will be gratified by the far reach of his influence on a fledgling novelist instead of compelled to contact his lawyers to pursue a copyright infringement suit for using his name and likeness without his expressed written consent. Livie's manifesto is really Jimmy's worldview in translation. I have been in the cheap seats at every Buffett show in Charlotte since 1993, waiting for the perfect deep cut from the almost forgotten album. I was fortunate enough to find the magic dust in those old songs at a very young age, and I think you'll notice it sprinkled liberally throughout this tale. Our island is always waiting—it's just up to us to plot our own escape.

ONE LITTLE SHRIMP
LONELY AND BLUE

Things went all cockeyed senior year in 1995 when Livie Green lost the homecoming crown by four votes to Augusta Lee Hammond, a certified hussy who offered the most unladylike sexual favors to the entire offensive line of the varsity football team in her shameless, but successful campaign to swing the election her way. The following Monday, Livie showed up to school wearing white shoes—in late October, mind you—a full two months after it was safe to do so in Avery, North Carolina, the tiniest dollop of an almost-coastal town near the Albemarle Sound. We were all freshly-minted débutantes, but we just knew the Junior League ladies would get word of Livie's transgression and have her excommunicated from the *Order of the Ladies Who Lunch*. For eighteen years, she had marched in a straight line with the rest of us, but that was the juncture at which our roads diverged. In secret, she started smoking cheap cigars—the kind the stoners used to roll weed—and reading poets none of us had ever heard of. Her senior thesis was on Ezra Pound's *Cantos,* a collection of poems our local library didn't even own and had to special order. Our AP English teacher couldn't follow the complexities of Livie's brilliant oral presentation about the significance of Pound's captivity in Pisa, Italy, and the segments of the *Cantos* he composed there. Livie was so many curves down the road ahead of us that we couldn't even see the glow of her taillights anymore. She acquired a taste for drinking Bud Light—the house wine of eastern NC—out of a can, taught herself to play the ukulele and earned the nickname "Live It Up Livie." In short, she simply rattled out of the mold much sooner and with much more force than any of us could conceive, and the potential consequences scared the bejesus out of us all—all except Livie.

When our clique of Baptist girls disbanded for college, most went to find husbands and pursue symbolic degrees in psychology and history that they hoped they would never have to use. I found my happy place in nursing school at Appalachian State University, and Livie, who graduated in the top five of our class at Avery High, hunkered down at the University of North Carolina to study literature, the only major she could think about without throwing up a little bit in her mouth.

By the merciful hand of God, she made it out of Carolina without becoming a left-wing robot programmed with a bunch of CNN talking points. I'll admit I was worried she'd come back a hairy-pitted feminist who somehow managed to insert the word "patriarchy" into even the most innocuous conversations. Our girl never even let her NRA card lapse while she was gone. She did, however, come away from the college experience with one ding on her record, a misdemeanor that really wasn't Carolina's fault, per se. One night she got arrested for being on the scene of a protest targeting a campus research facility that was doing unspeakable things to mice in the name of cutting-edge mascara science. While Livie's hands didn't actually set the fire that destroyed the cars of the lab assistants, she had no problem going to jail to achieve a modicum of justice for the animals. It felt good to know that the real rats got what they had coming. After driving to Durham and bailing her out in the wee hours of the morning, I decided to keep some extra cash on hand at the house just in case. I knew good and well that she was the only person on the planet who would ever bring a large sum of cash to a jail in the middle of the night for me without asking questions.

After graduation, Livie scored a sweet teaching assistantship in the English department at Chapel Hill and set about getting her Masters and Ph.D. straight through. Though it wasn't her intention to move back home, Livie pulled it off fast like a bandage after her final graduation. She'd been offered a job at Clary-Smith University, a Baptist private liberal arts school just outside of Greenville, NC. The salary wasn't much to speak of, but her only other job offers came from a state-supported school in Armpit, Arkansas, and a community college in Minnesota, an institution eighteen hours away from the ocean and covered in snow six months out of the year. Livie knew a fresher hell never existed than those two places, so Clary-Smith it was. Her selection incited very public jubilation on the part of Mama Green, who finally had her baby back home *and* teaching on a Baptist campus to boot.

Livie had a meager but reliable income, Mama was happy, and I had my best friend a few miles down the road again. But there were dangerous storm clouds rolling on the horizon that none of us detected, and when the shit hit the fan, it made the biggest mess you ever saw.

I'm Blair Chrisman, Livie's best friend since Avery First Baptist Church Vacation Bible School, 1982. Y'all aren't going to believe this story, but I swear it's true. I couldn't make it up if I tried.

BLAIR
So this guy came in the ER last
night with his wife.

LIVIE
Okay
So ...

So they had an unfortunate
accident ... with a pool noodle ...
in the bedroom.

Who exactly was in medical distress?
The him or the her?

Oh, it was definitely him. You
have never seen such agony.

I'm assuming he didn't swallow it.

Nope. Not with his mouth.
It went in so far that it broke off
in his abdomen.

Sweet Baby Jesus.

After 8 years in the ER, I was
fairly confident that I had seen it
all. I had not.

Were they dying of embarrassment?

Oh no. Not even an ounce
of shame.

Well dadgum. Who knew there were
so many perverts in rural NC?

We walk among them, sister.

From: Green, Olivia
Sent: Sunday, August 7, 2011 10:46 AM
To: Larsen, Holly
Subject: Monday Itinerary

Dr. Larsen,

Welcome to the Clary-Smith Fall Faculty Conference Self-Preservation Society. After receiving your nomination from Dr. Anderson, we are delighted to have you join us as we do our best to endure another week of mind-numbing and utterly useless meetings, workshops, and break-out sessions.

Attached you will find your card for Monday's round of Faculty Assembly Bingo. Winner takes all with a row of five connected up, down, or diagonally. The first one to text "BINGO" to our group thread will win the thirty-dollar pot.

Also, Dr. O'Brien has earned this year's "Get Out Of Meeting Free Card," which means it is her turn to skip a thirty-minute session of her choice by hiding in the bathroom and, if she is questioned by a member of the administration, using the excuse that the breakfast/lunch provided by the university did not settle well. Remember, too, that mimosas will be available in Dr. Cameron's mini-fridge during the morning session, and Jell-O shots will be offered in Dr. Burris's geology lab in the afternoon—all top secret, of course.

All the Best,
Dr. Olivia Green
FFCSPS Chair, 2011-2012
If We Couldn't Laugh, We Would All Go Insane

Fall Faculty Conference Self-Preservation Society BINGO

*All words in quotation marks must be uttered verbatim by a scheduled speaker.

"Innovation"	Dispute Settled with Robert's Rules	Dr. Turner Is 20 Mins. Late	"Welcome Back" – Fifth Time Only	Microphone Feedback
Coffee Runs Out / Dr. Ayers Complains from the Floor	"Collaboration"	We Are Put Into Small Groups to Reflect	"Student Success"	Someone at Your Table Is Really Reading a Book
"Retention"	Sound Doesn't Work on a Video Clip	FREE SPACE Dr. Tan's Ringer Wasn't Off	Announcement of New Enrollment Strategy	Dr. Harkey Objects to a Curricular Proposal
Revised Form Distributed (any kind)	Naïve Comment from New Faculty Member	Dr. Zink Asks President for a Raise	Room Is Freezing Ass Cold	Distressing Factoid about New Freshmen
"That's a Great Question" AND Speaker Doesn't Answer It	"Big Changes Are Coming"	CFO Doesn't Have That Information with Him	We Are Told What Our Personal Goals Should Be	Last Year's Bad Assessment Data Is Glossed

Clary-Smith University
Office of Human Resources

Memorandum

To: All Faculty and Staff
FROM: Denise Harper, Director of Human Resources
DATE: 15 August 2011
SUBJECT: Dress Code Policy Change

During the 2010-2011 academic year, Clary-Smith University retained the consulting services of Collegiate Resources for Academic Persistence, the nation's premier consulting firm for institutions of higher education interested in improving student retention.

After careful consideration, the senior administration team has decided to implement the central recommendation in the report recently delivered by the consulting liaisons to the Board of Trustees.

Effective immediately, employees are banned from wearing open-toe footwear on campus. This includes flip-flops, sandals, peep-toe, and "Croc" style shoes.

The only exception will be made for the assistant swimming coaches during periods of pool maintenance.

The Human Resources Department thanks you in advance for your cooperation with this policy and for your continued dedication to Clary-Smith's academic enterprise.

CC: Clary-Smith University Board of Trustees

LIVIE

BE BACK IN 10 MEETINGS

So I wrote this on my
office door today. Freudian slip.

BROTHER

I told you the Straight and
Narrow Way wasn't sustainable.

Oh, so you're a life coach now?

A steady stream of Southern
Comfort, a long line of women
with loose morals and a
consistent record of questionable
decision-making has worked for
me. Think on it. And take a day
off, Dr. Dumbass.

Stop calling me that.

Once she set her mind to finding Jimmy Buffett, we all knew that come hell or high water, Livie would follow through. After five years of teaching at Clary-Smith, she had lost her will to pretend she enjoyed it. She had played along like a champ, chairing multiple committees, gathering mountains of assessment data the administration would never read, publishing articles in the scholarly journals of her discipline, delivering presentations at prestigious academic conferences, attending university events ad nauseum, and generally kissing all of the asses that required it. Her mind began to wander during faculty meetings—to Caribbean beaches, pool bars, and palm-shaded cabanas staffed by servers who knew how to mix a drink. The legal pad her colleagues assumed contained the notes she would need to complete the minutes she was supposed to be taking was actually filling with the song lyrics that had hijacked her ability to concentrate. Harvesting the energy of hours and hours her co-workers had wasted paying attention in pointless meetings, Livie polished up what she was convinced was the perfect Jimmy Buffett song. Meeting him had always been on her bucket list, but a new impetus now drove her toward the goal.

Her dogged persistence in contacting him hadn't paid off yet. None of the addresses provided by the Parrot Head Fan Club actually connected to his desk in any way. Buffett's management company ignored her emails and blocked her calls. His recording label officially banned her from the property. Longtime Coral Reefer Mac McAnally had even taken out a restraining order against her after an episode that really wasn't one of her finer moments. The more detached she became from her job (especially after the HR memo about the new footwear policy inspired her to wear knee-high snow boots to work each day) the more intense her interest became in trying to reach Mr. Buffett. It was so hard watching her endure the sting of disappointment with each published newspaper article heralding another surprise visit he logged at a Key West bar, electrifying the unsuspecting crowd and lighting up Duval Street like a Roman candle. So many *If I had just been there's* reverberated in her spirit, each one adding to a growing wave of discontent that could only end in an epic crescendo. The question was not *if*—it was totally *when*.

BLAIR

I have been watching a Dog the Bounty Hunter marathon for so long that I am beginning to think Duane Chapman is hot. I can't stop thinking about running my fingers through his mullet.

LIVIE

You're talking to the girl who has a thing for crusty old Willie Nelson. I'm afraid I can't help you on this one, other than to suggest that you get off the couch and go outside for some fresh air.

That's right. I forgot.

What is wrong with us?

Nothing's wrong with us. We just get a little sideways every now and again.

The September night in 2011 that Livie began to unravel started with a colossal tower of first-year composition research papers. As she read yet another student essay that began with "In today's society," she felt compelled to gouge her eyeballs out with something sharp. In that moment, the simmer of the day's events reached a rolling boil: the reference letter request from a graduating senior written like a text message with no proper nouns capitalized; the notification that her conference funding application had been denied in committee because her dean forgot to include the date beside his signature on one of the six necessary forms; the telephone tirade from the angry father on behalf of his perfect little prince, who had just been convicted of plagiarism for copying and pasting a significant portion of the Wikipedia entry for William Carlos Williams' biography into his own essay without bothering to cite the source, change the font, *or* remove the hyperlinks; the meeting about the student who had somehow managed to maintain a zero average in his Literary Modernism course and the culminating decision by the department chair that Livie really should do more to "meet him where he is"—apparently at the corner of *Never Going to Hold a Job* and *Mom, Get the Basement Ready*. She had the self-awareness to realize that if she didn't unplug from university business for the night, she was in real danger of falling into a most undignified ugly cry.

She shoved the student essays off the edge of the bed in an unceremonious heap and stared at the uncharacteristic mess it created on her floor. Grading papers had consumed Livie's nights and weekends for the past decade, even though only a handful of her most industrious students bothered to read her meticulous and copious revision suggestions. The futility of it all piled on the most tender spot of her already shaky emotions. She eased back into a mound of pillows and began mindlessly surfing the cable channels, landing finally (after three rounds through the menu) on a hurricane preparedness special. It was the first hurricane season since Dr. Steve Lyons' retirement as The Weather Channel's longtime tropical specialist, and only a few minutes with the new doom-and-gloom crew (who basically insisted we were all going to die in a storm surge) revealed that Dr. Steve's brand of thoughtful and compelling commentary was no longer a network priority.

Zoning out and watching the spinning radar images of the monster cyclones of the past—including Hugo, which clobbered North Carolina when Livie was twelve—was surprisingly therapeutic, as long as the yakety-yak of the second-rate meteorologists was muted. Livie's mind easily drifted away from the day's pressures, and before long she realized she was humming "Trying to Reason with the Hurricane Season," Buffett's classic ode to Key West. The humming turned to singing and the singing then to strumming as she reached for her ukulele. She picked it up every six months or so, learned a few notes, and then promptly forgot them for lack of practice. Hesitantly, she progressed through the chords: the doable but weird D, the comfortable G, the funny E, and the easy A. When it was time for the chorus, she got caught up on the chickenshit B major, which required a finger spread her tiny hands couldn't maneuver. Not to be deterred, she kept going a capella:

And now I must confess, I could use some rest.

She stopped there and absorbed the timely message in those almost forty-year-old words. Then she landed back on her brother Carter's advice from earlier in the day: *I told you the Straight and Narrow Way wasn't sustainable.*

And that's when she saw it out of the corner of her eye: that withdrawn Saint Louis University Library edition of Walter C. Maloney's 1876 *Sketch of the History of Key West, Florida* that had been pushed to the side of her home office desk for months because of the crush of work obligations. She reached for it and her relief was immediate and euphoric. In an instant, she was transported back to the nineteenth century streets of the bustling island, surprisingly the largest city by population in Florida at the time. Through the hazy memories of a 1999 spring break trip that had now logged more than a decade in the dusty file folders of her mind, she tried to imagine the places Maloney described, the original buildings, the intrepid early citizens, and the genesis of perhaps the most curious city in America.

To say she devoured the book would be a gross understatement. Every sentence of Maloney's tome rained down on her in a shower of relief and escape. She could feel something breaking loose in her spirit, and the walls of her grandparents' old farmhouse, normally a place of solace, began to close in on her. She was overcome by the desire in that instant to buy a ticket on a southbound plane, but the post-it reminder on her day planner about the faculty meeting at ten the next morning slapped the foolhardy thought away.

That night, she slept an incredibly uncomfortable sleep, with tumultuous dreams shaking her each hour. She woke up damp with sweat in twisted sheets and blankets, her normal bedtime snuggle buddy, Mr. Don Ho the Cat, nowhere to be found. Unable to cast off her overwhelming feeling of dislocation, she ran her hands down the smooth brown binding of Maloney's book, which was still in the bed beside her where it fell when she finally succumbed to her fitful sleep. If ever there were a crossroads in a young woman's life, this was it. If she had to sit through one more academic meeting that should have been an email instead, she knew she was at risk of hurting herself (or, more likely, one of her colleagues). It was difficult to comprehend how a room of people with such a collective storehouse of knowledge could be so ineffectual—and have absolutely no clue about it. She stared at the numbers on the clock that announced the twenty-eight minutes she had left before she was required to hop into the shower to make her meeting. Twenty-one minutes. Sixteen. Ten. Her fingernails tapped the cover of the book. Six minutes. Two minutes. *Beep. Beep. Beep.*

Mama Green always knew Livie would pay for having her head in the clouds and her nose in a book. Her baby girl's name wouldn't be on the meeting attendance roster today.

She packed just the essentials into her 1993 Mercedes 190E: flip-flops, bikinis, a beach chair, her ukulele, an assortment of suntan lotions and oils, a few toiletries, a suitcase with enough summer clothes to last a month, a bag of books she really wanted to read, and Don Ho's cat carrier. She tucked her natural blonde curls into a knot at the nape of her neck and didn't bother with any makeup. At seven fifteen a.m., she made the right turn out of her grandparents' gravel driveway and onto the highway. Realizing that in her distraction she'd pulled right slap out in front of an oncoming car, she was forced to make the turn with haste, goosing the accelerator, slinging a few rocks, and feeling very much a part of her own *Thelma & Louise* moment.

From underneath her passenger-side seat slid her long-lost copy of disc one of Jimmy Buffett's *You Had to Be There*. It was a sign, a tangible confirmation that her old car was pointed in the right direction. She quickly skipped ahead to track three—"Wonder Why We Ever Go Home"—and let Don Ho out of the pokey. He assumed his rightful position on the cashmere pashmina he had claimed with his vomit the day Livie brought home her new luxury from Neiman Marcus after saving for four months to buy it. He knew he was a bastard for doing such a thing, but he convinced himself that he made up for it with a whole array of other fine personal qualities. Perhaps the pissiest animal to ever draw breath on this earth, he had been dumped at a kill shelter as a kitten, and he had never forgotten the indignity.

In protest of Livie's absence for work each day, he kicked the litter out of his pan and hid his little kitty cat turds like Easter eggs all over the house. Luckily, he was a most agreeable car rider—as long as an Allman Brothers CD was in rotation. He had been deeply moved by *Eat a Peach* in the early years of his life, and by the time he and Livie crossed the South Carolina line, he was already cutting his big green eyes at her in his plea for an album change. "Revival," track one from *Idlewild South,* did the trick.

Facing a freedom ride of fifteen hours, she shot down I-95 like she was driving a getaway car. She waited until she reached the Florida/Georgia line to call her sweet Daddy and tell him she was taking an extended break from work for the rest of the semester. She promised to call him once an hour with the interstate mile marker she'd just passed. Otherwise, his worry would turn into hours of nervous diarrhea due to her making such a long drive alone.

Before she'd left home, she decided to splurge, booking herself a real trip for the first time in her adult life. She realized then the disservice she had done to herself for failing to pay attention to the impact of fifteen years of physical, intellectual, and emotional exhaustion. Living rent-free on her grandparents' property had allowed her to amass a nice stack of cash in her savings account, yet the thought of using some of it for a mission-of-mercy vacation hadn't even crossed her mind. Two weeks at the Casa Marina hotel in Key West—one week to play and one week to figure out what the hell she was going to do about things—would serve as her personal mea culpa. She had confidence that the UVA/UVB rays, the cocktails, and the salt air would help her devise a plan.

LIVIE

I'm eating fresh Georgia shrimp
with my toes in the ocean.

BLAIR

Okay. Not cool. I'm eating a
bologna sandwich in the break
room. What have you gotten
yourself into, chica?

Heading down 95.
It would be a homemade sin to
be this close to the coast and
not stop for fried shrimp.

Spur of the moment vacay?

You could say that. I'll call
you tonight and explain.

Okey-dokey. Safe travels.

*M*ama Green was on the warpath. Her shorts began to twist the day she was informed that Livie was not finished with college after her undergraduate matriculation and intended to pursue a Masters degree.

"Olivia June," she pleaded, "I'm proud of you for going to college and all, but no man is interested in a dangerously over-educated woman. It's just not normal. Graduate school will be the kiss of death for your marriage prospects." Not to be dissuaded, Livie persisted right on through her Ph.D. The degradation with which Mama informed her prayer group of Livie's doctoral dissertation topic (Ernest Hemingway and alcohol) was palpable in the Sunday School room that day. All those old bags shook their heads in solemn disbelief as if Mama had just informed them that Livie had dropped her drawers on the courthouse lawn and given the whole town a free show.

Since the day Livie turned fifteen, she had been secretly betrothed in Mama's mind to Randy Parsons, a sad twenty-something who wore the most regrettable short-sleeved dress shirts and ran the church sound board for the contemporary service at eleven a.m. If Mama had her druthers, Randy would have volunteered instead for the early traditional service, which was scheduled for the old and almost dead at eight thirty a.m. Truth be told, Mama didn't know what went on at that eleven o'clock service, though she had long suspected punk rock music was involved. One of the elders' wives had nearly fainted the day the drum set first appeared behind the pulpit. All bets were off in a service for people who were too lazy to get up and praise the Lord at a reasonable hour. Despite Mama's repeated rejoinder that Randy had a new KIA Forte, a stable job at an insurance agency, and absolutely no nasty baggage from past relationships (because he'd never been in one, bless his heart), Livie's romance with Randy had never materialized. Instead, she had opted in her first graduate semester at Carolina to date Steve, a Yankee agnostic with libertarian political leanings. To compound the disgrace, Livie then decided to live in sin with Steve in an off-campus apartment that Mama refused to fund. When news of the horror reached Avery and the church hens began clucking, Mama had taken to bed for two weeks to hide out and attempt (unsuccessfully but not for lack of trying) to die from humiliation.

Because our merciful Lord is always in control, Livie's relationship with Steve had met its inevitable end, at which point she began seeing Zachary. He was nice—nice to Livie, nice in conversation, nice in helping out around Livie's apartment—and he hung in there all the way through the terminal degree. Livie, sure that a proposal was imminent after more than five years of uncomplicated but dreadfully boring dating, had lately come to realize that Zachary only had one oar in the water, and the idea of being stuck in his circling dinghy for the rest of her life was the stuff of nightmares. So a few weeks ago, she'd done the humane thing and nipped it in the bud. Old Zach took it as one would expect: nicely.

Now Mama's knickers were in a complete and unrelenting knot. Innocently enough, Daddy had told her about Livie's call, about the break she was taking from the university. Mama zeroed in like a hawk circling a nest of freshly born baby squirrels. *This was no vacation.* She knew it deep in her bones. And her Mama radar was on it.

The southbound driver who makes it through the mind-numbing cluster that is the Homestead/Miami area is richly rewarded by the sight of the aqua blue median wall that divides the A1A between Florida City and Key Largo. Mirroring the reflection of the azure waters that begin to peek through the mangroves on this captivating stretch of highway, the turquoise paint scheme is wholly unexpected. It's easy to imagine the day the Florida Department of Transportation worker was told to go out there and paint that cement wall. He made the choice to depart from the anticipated DOT yellow, a color not fitting of the tropical panorama that unfolds on either side of the Overseas Highway. His gift is the traveler's first indication that something unusual and wondrous awaits.

"Hey, Daddy," said Livie as she continued south.

"Hey, Baby Doll. Listen, I know you tried to call Mama a few days ago, but I think she's ready to talk now. Why don't you give it another go?"

"I promise, I'll do it today."

"You know she would take a bullet for you. She just struggles when she doesn't feel like she's in the know with what's happening."

"I can't explain my reasons just yet because I don't really understand, but I know this is something I need to do," Livie explained. "I didn't even think about how alarming this would be for y'all. I'll call her in a little bit."

"That'll help her. Did you change your oil before you left on your wild goose chase? You know the Merc has been burning a lot of oil lately."

"I did, Daddy."

"And do you still have that road atlas I put in your car?"

"Yes sir, and the maps of all the Southern states are still bookmarked."

"What about the fire extinguisher?"

"I never take it out of the trunk, Daddy."

"That's my girl."

BROTHER

Livs. What in the Sam hell?

LIVIE

The weather is here.
I wish you were beautiful!

You haven't joined a
cult, have you?

After watching that Scientology
documentary? Lord no.

I'm afraid we're going to
have to hog-tie Mama and put her
on an involuntary hold down at
the clinic. This is even worse than that
time I got caught spray-painting
pornographic stick figure scenes on the
side of the church van. CALL HER!

Doing it now.

"Hey, Butter Bean," Mama Green said flatly.

"Hey, Mama."

The tension was apparent, and Livie knew with the slightest misstep, Mama would make her feel like she had walked face first into a weed-eater.

"Dad told me you made it to Florida in one piece. I'm relieved," Mama Green said.

"I did. And I really am sorry for not keeping you in the loop. A clean break was absolutely necessary, and I didn't know that until everything actually broke loose."

"So, how long are you going to be down there?"

"At least two weeks, I know, because that's how long I booked the hotel. I'm hoping to find an apartment and a job."

"I just don't understand your attraction to that place, Olivia. It's a big old jumble of drunken spring breakers, ungodly humidity, and voodoo all caught up in a cloud of cigarette smoke. I bet there isn't even a church down there."

"Mama, there has been a bona fide Baptist church on the island since 1848. It's older than Avery Baptist, in fact. And on Sunday I visited a Four Square Church that is really a lot of fun. The pastor is young, and most of the congregation is, too."

"Is the preacher married?" Mama prodded.

"Good Lord, Mother. Yes. He's married—with kids. He moved here from Puerto Rico a few years ago. His sermon on Sunday was inspired and anointed."

"Well, you just never know about preachers from exotic places. He's not sacrificing goats out back or anything, is he? Are you being asked to handle snakes?"

"No, actually most of the snake-handling churches are confined to the service roads in rural North Carolina. Very little danger of that down here in the tropics," Livie assured her.

"Baby, I just don't know how you're going to make it alone so far from home. I'm worried. Do they even sell grits at the grocery store?"

"Mama, they sell grits …."

"Don't even finish that sentence, girl, because I know what you're going to say. 'They have Quaker Quick Grits.'"

Mama believed that instant grits were an abomination that no self-respecting Southerner would ever be caught consuming. If they weren't ground by a mill stone way below the Mason-Dixon line, those grits weren't crossing the threshold of the Green house. A major point of contention in their mother/daughter relationship stemmed from the fact that Livie was not a grits purist, a truth she could never acknowledge because she knew what the consequences would be.

"Do they at least have sweet tea?" Mama pleaded.

"No, but there is always ample sugar on the table."

"And how do you plan to find a lady doctor to handle your gynecology? I guarantee you every OB on that island is a slick rascal who oozed down from Miami to prey on nice young girls like you. It's just not fitting to ask a man to remain objective and focused while he's working *down there.*"

"Mama, please. I was due for my yearly exam, so I already made an appointment for next week at a little practice in Old Town. They have a female doctor, but her schedule was full, so I'm seeing one of the male doctors just this one time. He's perfectly qualified, and I can assure you that there is nothing so spectacular about my hoo-ha that he won't be able to remain objective and focused while he assesses its well-being," Livie quipped.

"Well, you don't listen to anything else I say, so this one doesn't come as a surprise either. You were raised to know better, and I have said my piece. What day is your appointment?"

"It's Friday, but Mama don't tell your prayer group about this. Betty Varner can't keep her mouth shut about anything. I'm tired of hearing from people that my prayer request has been on their heart lately—all while I haven't been making any prayer requests. Y'all should change the name of that group from the 'Prayer Warriors' to the 'Baptist Gossip Association.'"

"We do the best we can to serve the Lord and help others. If you don't appreciate our prayers, then that's on you. In other news, did I tell you that Tiffani Triplett had a Tupperware party the other night?"

Tiffani Triplett, secretly known as "Tiffani Titless" by her junior high bullying victims (Livie and I included), had all of the church ladies suckered from the moment she emerged from the womb like a precious little lamb. Her nail polish was never chipped. Her hemlines were always perfectly modest, with a few extra inches to spare. She took pride in having her hand in the air first—to fill in the blank with the correct word during the scripture game in Sunday School, to volunteer to lead a mission trip in search of lost souls deep in the Tennessee hills, to vote for herself on any number of school and church committees. All of the parents saw a generous, pious, and darn near flawless young lady in Tiffani and wondered aloud why their kids couldn't take a lesson from her and at least pretend like they were raised right.

"Tiffani's get-together was something to see," Mama continued. "She served these miniature tacos in tiny baked tortilla bowls, and we just couldn't get enough of them. Absolutely everybody from the church was there, and they all asked me where you were. I didn't know what to say about my very own daughter to my very own friends."

"First of all, if they're your friends, you can tell them the truth. Secondly, Tiffani Triplett has suckered you into every home party Ponzi scheme that has breezed through Avery in the last decade. She will do anything to get y'all in her house so you can spend an evening complimenting her decorating choices, her finger foods, and her unblemished moral virtue, all while she guilts you into buying overpriced things. It's disgraceful."

"Now, Olivia …."

"It's true. Don't tell me your fifty-five dollar Ordinary Otter locket didn't snap like a macaroni necklace the second time you wore it. It's not rude to decline the repeated invitation to have yourself taken advantage of, Mama. You don't need a consultant to buy a candle for the bathroom."

"Wait just a hot minute here. If you want to talk about rude, let's put on our big girl panties and walk down that road for a spell. How would you classify moving out of state under the cover of night without breathing a word of it to your mother?"

"I've clearly not met my apology quota yet. I'm sincerely sorry, Mama."

"Well, we'll get through it. You call me every day, now, and your Daddy, too. His stomach is still not right from fretting over you driving to Florida by yourself. He's been drinking Pepto-Bismol every hour on the hour."

"I'll call, Mama. I promise."

"You know I love you more than life, girl. Be safe down there."

"I love you, Mama."

LIVIE

Is it standard procedure for a
gynecologist to stick his finger up
your butt hole (without warning)
during a yearly exam?

BLAIR

Ummmm. No. Not really. Never.

I didn't think so ... was just
asking for a friend.

*M*aking a two-week reservation at the Casa Marina on Reynolds Street was, without question, the best life choice Livie ever made. For seven straight September Floridays, she staked a claim on her preferred beach chair, instructed the waiters at the pool bar to keep the banana coladas coming, and drifted like an aimless manatee on a floating chaise lounge that felt like a cloud. Dark rum, fresh bananas, and coconut crème coalesced in the blender to yield the precise frozen concoction Livie needed to medicate her parched soul. The khaki-clad pool servers—attentive to Livie's overdue vacation affliction—anticipated her need for chilled washcloths and mango popsicles. Livie knew for sure that she was approaching the kind of spoiled one never recovers from, and she hugged that thought tight with both arms.

On the eighth day, Livie retired her bikini, put on actual clothes—a saucy sundress and white sandals that accentuated the coffee color of her new tan—and walked into Old Town. On her way down Duval Street for the first time in twelve years, she met a smiling golden retriever wearing sunglasses and trotting at a brisk pace in the opposite direction. No collar. No leash. No owner in sight. Just going about his island business like everyone else.

Her first stop was a vacation rental office on Simonton Street. A job ad in the *Conch Telegraph* sought a responsible property manager for an exclusive ten-unit condo complex on Emma Street called Mills Place in the gated community of Truman Annex, the swankiest neighborhood in Key West. Apparently, the position had been open for quite some time, but the Ph.D. on Livie's curriculum vitae did its job and caught the eye of the office manager, who was weary of screening hundreds of fruitless applicants who tried but failed to convey their trustworthiness. The owner of the property was hoping to market the complex to visiting writers and artists looking for a very quiet and posh space to work. In exchange for serving as the on-call property manager twenty-four hours a day and cleaning the units after the long-term tenants checked out, Livie would get to live rent free in the small, but fully-furnished, waterfront apartment on the second story of the two-car garage and use one of the parking spaces. In the land of Key West real estate, where the rents are high and even respectable folks will cut you with a shank over an open parking space, Livie had just scored the Holy Grail of living arrangements. Maybe the Baptist Gossip Association's fervent intercession for her passage through this heathen land was actually moving the needle in her favor.

Her next appointment was with Flit Williams, the curmudgeonly heavy-weight-boxer-turned-bar-manager of the Schooner Wharf, Old Town's only twenty-four hour watering hole. With happy hour specials beginning at seven a.m. and breakfast at seven thirty, the Wharf was the place to be in the morning. Livie suspected her bartending experience at Durham's TGI Fridays in graduate school in combination with her easy laugh and her D-cup breasts sealed the deal with Flit, who was completely done with filling in on the early morning shift since the last waitress quit two months ago. He offered her the job on the spot with a sigh of relief.

Just like that, Livie had a roof over her head and gainful (if slightly sketchy) employment. Mama was going to have a dying duck fit when she found out Livie was working in a bar again, but like a modern-day Scarlett O'Hara, that was a problem she'd face another day. She went back to the Casa Marina to tell Don Ho they were moving on up to a deluxe apartment in Truman Annex. He accepted the news with reluctance, as he had grown very fond of the ray of almost equatorial sunshine that shone on his afternoon napping pallet. The promise of a porch facing the ocean where pots of fresh catnip could be grown did pique his interest, though.

LIVIE

Walmart in Key West is selling
banana clips. 1987 is circling
the wagons on us.

BLAIR

You are in the liquor.
Buy me two of them.

Already had them in the cart.

*L*ivie's first week at the Wharf was not all rainbows and puppy toes. Unaccustomed to the second-hand smoke, she developed a fiendish sinus infection, the kind of sick that forces even mass quantities of Sudafed to wave the white flag of defeat. The physicality of the job also made her acutely aware of her thirty-four years. The last time she tended bar was more than a decade ago when she was a perky sprite of twenty-one. She was now discovering that her muscles didn't spring back so easily from the hours spent bending over beer coolers to load ice and bottles. Huffing eucalyptus oil by day and soaking in peppermint oil baths by night, she was dragging like a very old bag of rocks.

Luckily, the morning crew at the Wharf (both staff and customers) was a hoot and a half. Livie was almost always scheduled to work with Rita, a fifty-something who had been employed at the Wharf since she was Livie's age. Rita was seasoned like the best kind of cast iron skillet, and once she decided she liked Livie, Rita taught her how to make her infamous Pain Killers, the drink that brought many a local into the Wharf after a night of over-indulgence. The key was the extra shot of rum that you had to slide in there when Flit wasn't looking. Hector the line cook could sing just like Ricky Ricardo, and he spent the morning flipping the Wharf's legendary pancakes and belting out "Babalu" and "Guadalajara." The patrons, a healthy mix of regulars and the good kind of tourists, were rarely rowdy on Livie's six thirty a.m. to three p.m. shift, and she quickly realized she would rather pour drinks for them than deal with the lunacy that higher education seemed to be descending into.

Her shift hours made it possible to go back to Mills Place and either take a nap or clean vacant apartment units before she circulated among the downtown bars just in case Buffett happened to pop into one. Judging by his past visits, the most likely site for a surprise concert was the Margaritaville Café on Duval. Most unfortunately, it was almost always populated by morons walking around in grass skirts and pirate hats and waiting for "Margaritaville" to cycle back around on the sound system because they knew the words and could sing along and feel proud of themselves for it. Livie endured night after night at the bar, but the cynical (yet accurate) words of Carter, eight years her senior, always echoed in her head: *Jimmy Buffett hasn't made a true Jimmy Buffett album since 1981's* Coconut Telegraph.

The real fans recognized his musical peak and turned their attention instead to his wonderful fiction, the arena that in the 1990s and 2000s was getting the lion's share of his creative energy. Livie and Carter weren't Parrot Heads— they were Buffett aficionados who recognized the genius of his earliest albums. They tolerated "Margaritaville" at the concerts just as much as Jimmy seemed to. Poor guy had to be tired of singing it night after night when it could have been replaced in the set list with a gem like "I Heard I Was in Town" or "When the Coast Is Clear." The simple-minded vacationers with their coconut shell bikini tops and inflatable shoulder parrots wouldn't understand that at all. Livie just wanted to talk to him for a minute. She was convinced that one day it would happen. She just had to wait her turn.

Soon after taking the Wharf job, Livie accepted what turned out to be a one-time date with an oyster shucker at Pepe's Café on Caroline Street. Darrell bought her an incredibly tasty and fairly expensive hogfish sandwich from B.O.'s Fish Wagon before she discovered that it was his belief that buying her a seafood dinner obligated her to deliver an untoward act of sexual renumeration in return. Upon her refusal to comply and his accusation that she was nothing but a "mainland tease," Livie made it known that he had two options: A) apologize sincerely and get out of her line of sight or B) be subdued with the taser gun she quickly took out of her purse while she called her Daddy back in North Carolina, who would charter an aircraft and find a way to arrive on the island within the hour along with his trusty shotgun. Her Daddy had, after all, shot men for lesser offenses in the very recent past. Sufficiently convinced that this was the way backwoods NC crazy rolled, the young oyster shucker offered his most heartfelt apologies and never came into the Wharf again. Livie then realized that Key West girls apparently don't stand up for themselves. She was going to have to have a word with them about this.

The slow weekday mornings at the Wharf were quiet enough to hear the pelicans honking at each other on the dock. On breaks, Livie had time to dangle her feet over the pier at the bight and watch the tarpon glide between the parked boats. Sometimes she would take a pocket journal with her and try to sift through all of the thoughts swirling in her head, the first personal writing she'd done since high school. As the only cool Key West breezes that would pass through on those days kissed Livie's warm shoulders, she stared out to the point where the calm blue water touched the sky and savored her long, deep breaths. What a funny feeling it was to exhale the garbage and inhale the stuff of imagination all in one sitting.

```
THE BIKE SHOP OF KEY WEST
      1110 TRUMAN AVENUE
     KEY WEST, FL 33040


BICYCLE VINTAGE LIME        199.99
HANDLEBAR BASKET             24.99
REAR WICKER BASKET           45.99
SALES TAX                    18.97

              TOTAL: $289.94

    SERVING KW SINCE 1981
         THANK YOU
```

"Blair Bear. Bad news," said Livie when I answered.
"Ruh-roh," I said in my best Scooby Doo voice.

"I totally wrecked the Merc this morning."

"Oh, holy night. Are you okay?"

"I'm fine, just flustered and a little bit sore. The silver lining is that I got a great story out of it. I was driving down Whitehead Street right in front of the post office, and this assemblage of unruly roosters was fighting with each other. They looked like they were going to spill off the sidewalk and out into the road. So ... I was watching them instead of the car stopped at the intersection ahead of me."

"I don't have any use for a disorderly rooster," I added.

"Nor do I. So the car I rear-ended—a tank of a 1970s Pontiac—that was the real adventure. It had to be the last of its breed on the road. The best part—it was painted

1980 Barbie Dream House Swimming Pool blue with about 200 conch shells epoxied all over it."

"Oh! That was such a good year. And that was the best Dream House ever," I said.

"At that point, the rooster quarrel had moved into the roadway and escalated into a full-blown altercation, and all the folks on the sidewalk waiting to get their picture made with the Mile 0 marker were fully invested both in the bird calamity and the crash. As I walked up to the driver's door, a magnificent cloud of unfiltered Marlboro smoke encircled me. The driver was dragging on her cig like she was impatient for the emphysema, and if the empties on her seat were any indication, she had just about crushed a six-pack of Budweiser heavies. Our conversation was brief:

Her: 'I don't give a shit if you don't give a shit.'
Me: 'I don't give a damn.'

"Not wanting to get out of her car (this was clearly a Long Titty/No Bra Scenario), she asked if I would mind handing her the bottle of Jack Daniels that slid onto the floorboard from the passenger seat on impact. Of course, I obliged and then apologized profusely. She drove away, and I called a tow truck. And that, dear friend, is how car wrecks are handled in the Conch Republic."

"So what's the damage on the Merc?"

"Oh, she's toast. It will definitely cost more to fix her than she's worth. But no worries. I already have a new set of wheels: A Huffy Panama Jack bike with front and rear wicker baskets, a drink holder, and a bike bell that's cute as a bug's butt. I didn't really need a car down here anyway, but it sure is hard to say goodbye to a trusty old pal."

"She was an institution," I said. "I'm really sorry for your loss."

"Oh well. Onward and upward. I've put a little bit of junk in the trunk since I moved here, so maybe biking everywhere will help me lose a few pounds."

"And if not, there's always Richard Simmons," I reminded her. "I still have 'Sweatin' to the Oldies' on VHS. Holler if you need it."

LIVIE

I'm at Margaritaville having a beer.

BROTHER

What the hell for? You are
surrounded by 100 cooler
places to drink.

The man beside me just
ordered a Cheeseburger in Paradise.

Well done, right?

Yup. That's the guy. When the
bartender asked if he wanted
anything else, he broke into song:
"I like mine with lettuce and tomato,
Heinz 57 and French fried potatoes."

Did you punch him in the throat?

No, but I considered it.

*E*arly morning revelations are the best kind. Livie sped through the empty streets of Old Town with the determination of a six-year-old set on running away from home. Decades of worry, stress, and exhaustion released and evaporated into the humid air as she pedaled with increasing speed, turning her unruly curls into a tangled mess of ridiculousness. She was either *on the run* or *on the trail*. Only time would tell.

LIVIE

Blair Bear, do you remember that
time in junior high when my
dad pulled up to the McDonald's
drive-thru and ordered a
"mater sammich with
extra napkins" to embarrass us?

BLAIR

As I recall, we curled up in
the back floorboard and hid
our faces to shield ourselves
from the humiliation.

Hahahaha!

Feeling homesick?

A little bit—for people,
not necessarily place.

Thinking of coming
back for a visit?

No. In time maybe,
but not right now.

When she was in need of an extra-long break from Wharf duty, Livie would bike the few blocks over to Mallory Square to watch the evolution of the ocean's color as the clouds and the sun decided what they were going to do for the day. When time permitted, she would take advantage of the chance to browse the nearby Key West Historic Sculpture Garden minus the crowds. Reading the plaques affixed to the busts of Key West's most prominent movers and shakers stirred in Livie a great excitement for the peculiar and rich history of her new home. Maloney's book, which she still picked up from time to time, made her feel even more like the people from those long-ago days were reaching out to her.

The 1951 movie "The African Queen" was Mama Green's absolute favorite. When she would get mad at Daddy for doing something insensitive like failing to notice she'd gotten a new haircut, she would start the movie in the living room, turn up the volume to a few ticks past deafening, and offer thundering commentary about how nice Humphrey Bogart's "Charlie" was to Katharine Hepburn's "Rose." Carter and Livie would always snicker at the charade, which usually ended with Daddy settling in on the couch beside Mama and tickling her under the blanket, but Livie actually paid enough attention to the film to see why Mama loved it so much. Rose, an indomitable woman, navigated the perils of the Ulanga River with Charlie and refused to take no for an answer on much of anything. She knew what she wanted, and she made it happen. The actual boat used in the making of the film is docked at the Key Largo Holiday Inn Complex at Mile Marker 100.

The grip of the impending installment of Fantasy Fest was tightening on Old Town. "Aquatic Afrolic" was the chosen theme, and stores as far up as Key Largo had already sold out of body paints that paralleled the colors of the sea. It was a warm October afternoon, and Livie had just served a bucket of Rolling Rock to some locals who were preparing to leave town for the week to escape the chaos when a dark-haired man in his sixties with a full wooly goatee and a guitar strapped to his back pulled up to the bike rack outside the bar.

He walked over to Livie's post in search of a cup of ice water before his set began.

"I'm the talent for this afternoon. Mack Mason."

Extending her hand over the bar, she offered a chirpy, "Livie Green. Nice to meet you, sir."

"Hmmm. A pretty new girl in a good mood. The universe is clearly trying to get my attention."

"Ha! I started working here a few weeks ago. They haven't beaten the optimism out of me yet."

"Welcome, Livie Green."

The four people who were left after the breakfast rush were hung over and miserable, a very tough crowd for a one-man band. Earlier Livie had overheard one of them retching painfully in the bathroom, and under the stall door she offered him a Coca-Cola on ice, her Nana's tried and true remedy for tummy troubles.

"We've now reached the crowd participation segment of our program," Mack announced after several songs that ended with only a smattering of weak applause. "This next number has proven over the years to be both a crowd-pleaser and a toe-tapper. Does anyone in the house happen to know the whistling solo to Paul Simon's 'Me and Julio Down by the Schoolyard?' Anyone?"

Livie was listening to the show on the back deck on her lunch break. Mack was a very skilled guitar player—far better than any she'd heard on the island. The silence that followed his question was uncomfortable and unwarranted because everybody knows Paul Simon is awesome under every set of circumstances.

Without hesitation, she shouted, "I've got it!" as she stood up.

Mack began to play with new zeal as Livie walked through the almost empty bar and ascended the stage. The happiness of the tune immediately injected the Wharf with a jolt of positive energy, bringing in ten or twelve newcomers who wanted to be part of whatever was going down. When Livie commenced to whistle, Hector came out of the kitchen to twirl Rita around the dance floor, which was just the cue the growing crowd needed to get to their feet. The jubilation of their dancing was contagious, and they hopped around the bar like natives in a ceremonial boogie. Flit observed it all like a big stone wall, but he didn't have that look on his face like he'd just smelled poop, which was as close to a smile as he was probably ever going to get.

When the song ended to enthusiastic applause, it was time for the reggae band that was scheduled as the first act of Fantasy Fest to begin setting up.

Mack and Livie fell into an easy conversation back at the bar.

"I hear the Carolinas in that accent," he said.

"Eastern North Carolina."

"I also sense an education—and a good story."

"A doctorate. Hemingway specialist. Story unfolding. To be determined."

"What a wonderful coincidence. In addition to playing sparsely attended gigs all over town, I'm a groundskeeper at Hemingway's house and an ad hoc member of the Itty Bitty Kitty Committee on the property. The cats look to me as their human pack leader, mainly because I pack extra cold cuts in my lunch to share. You should come over sometime after the tourists leave, and the staff and I can give you the private tour."

"You don't have to twist my arm on that one, Mack Mason. Thanks."

LIVIE
My Mama would roll
over and die – and so would yours.
I just mixed a Bloody Mary for an
80-year-old man wearing nothing
but chaps, a pair of fairy wings, and
what can only be described as a
leather sleeve over his tallywacker.

BLAIR
What in the Wide World
of Sports?

Fantasy Fest. Before he came in,
I served a herd of body-painted zebras.
That's all they had on. Body paint.

Please let me tell Tiffani Triplett.
She would have an aneurysm,
and I would pay good money to
watch it happen.

Don't you dare. She'll tell her
Mama, who will tell my Mama that I'm
working in a bar and selling
alcoholic beverages to naked people.

*I*n 1937's *To Have and Have Not*, Ernest Hemingway depicted Key West as an island of stark contrasts— the extravagant yachts anchored beside the lowly fishing boats, the temporary tourists living high on the hog for a week or two, and those in it for the long haul trying to make it from paycheck to paycheck and supplementing income by any means necessary. The tropical ease and its seedy underbelly coexisted in the most delicate of truces. All of the Key West caricatures Hemingway crafted had one thing in common: they were searching people. As Livie adjusted to the island's cadence, she realized the same conditions still held true. Everyone was on a personal expedition. Key West was and is a haven for silly hearts and drifters, a little dab of salty earth full of promise and possibility and hope. What she didn't yet know was how many of them actually found what they were seeking.

Mack Mason was a reluctant wanderer, one who was forced into his journey rather than choosing it. After a brief but satisfying stint as a session musician in Nashville in the late 1960s and 70s, he left for greener pastures (and much bigger paychecks) in Houston. His brand new fiancé expected more of a lifestyle than his scant and unreliable paychecks from the country labels could provide, so at her insistence, he enrolled in college and began working his way up through the business ranks. After completing his MBA in the 1980s, he joined a little company called Enron, where his wife was immediately energized by his swelling bank account. The banal nature of his desk job, however, turned him into an insufferable grouch who his wife only barely tolerated in between shopping trips. The crash in 2001 was particularly painful for him: twenty-five years of savings wiped away just a year before he planned to retire early at fifty-five.

In his anguish, he embraced the realization that he would become a full-fledged asshole—at least for the time being. Instead of searching for an alternative plan of employment, Mack retreated to his man cave in the rear of his garage, teaching himself to play the trumpet with YouTube tutorials and rolling fat, tight doobies. In a haze of pot smoke one especially gloomy January afternoon, an epiphany struck him with great force and certainty: He was to become an artist, though he hadn't held a paintbrush since elementary school. He chose plain old paper as his canvas and colored pencils and markers as his medium, spending his days sketching immature island scenes that were especially funny when he was high. He found more pleasure than he had ever known in his mediocre horn playing, his even more mediocre folk art, and his most perfect joints.

His big idea to get the family out of financial turmoil was to find a publisher interested in transforming his sketch collections into adult coloring books. The pitch was simple: coloring reduces stress and is much cheaper than therapy. "The Shrew," as she had come to be known by this point, literally laughed in his face, hired the nastiest divorce lawyer in Houston, and put her full effort into taking everything he had left. Though he had worked hard his entire adult life toward owning that house, he didn't give a flying flip when she yanked the deed—now in her name—right out of his hand. With his evacuation orders from the court all written up, he had a choice to make. The load of airline miles glistening in his pocket like so many pearls made it an easy call. He determined that the rest of his life would be devoted to the singular pursuit of his own personal joy. He flew into Miami and took the next two years to inch his way south, stopping in every town in the Florida Keys and staying absolutely as long as he wanted to. His arrival in Key West in 2005 served as the climax of his extended mental blowout. It was an ideal place to finish losing his mind and to set about the business of finding it again.

*L*ivie was thoroughly exhausted from Fantasy Fest. For seven straight days, Old Town's bartenders had been busier than a clutter of cats covering crap on a marble floor. Even so, Livie couldn't sleep for the first time since the night before she left home. It was eerie, and she didn't like the feeling one bit. She got up earlier than usual for a bike ride around the island. Old Town speaks a different language in the morning hours when the sun is just stretching from sleep and the sky begins its metamorphosis from Gulf Stream cerulean to Carolina blue. The sense of renewal Livie usually experienced in these quiet hours before all of Key West jumped out of bed was not to be found this morning. She could feel the stir of something different. The island wind was teaching her to listen, to pay attention, and to be ready. Always an astute learner, Livie recognized that something was about to shift.

Livie got into the Wharf early to help clean up the hideous post-Fantasy Fest mess left behind by what had to be 100,000 trashed revelers. As Livie locked her bike on the Williams Street rack, she noticed a hooptie of an old white Ford F-250 (with a camper top and giant cooler in the bed) parked at the delivery bay. The fading logo on the side—Stock Island Shrimp Company—was one she'd never seen at the Wharf before.

Once inside, all that eerie *blowing in the wind* stuff made sense.

The rear view alone was worth writing home about. It had to be said: His backside was just the right amount of wrong. Even in ragged khaki shorts, that much was clear. Respect was due, and Livie paid it in full while Hector signed the paper on the clipboard to complete the delivery receipt. He was in the neighborhood of six foot three— tall enough to get things down off of high shelves for you and tall enough to show any pair of pants he put on what was up. He had dark curly hair with the most tantalizing gray hairs streaking in over his ears to announce his approach to age forty without apology. Once he turned around to walk back through the bar to his truck, Livie was reasonably sure she had a little bit of an orgasm. He had weak-in-the-knees green eyes, a perpetual tan from the kiss of the Stock Island sun, and the strongest chiseled forearms Livie had ever seen. There was no ring on the important finger, just a strange gold coin suspended from a chain around his neck. It looked for the world like a piece of Spanish treasure from the pirate lore that had captured Livie's imagination since she learned to read.

"Don't get your hopes up." Livie's lust had not gone unnoticed by Rita. "You'd have better luck hitting on a brick wall."

"Hot spit. Who is he?"

"Luke. Stock Island shrimper. Flit has decided to put better shrimp on the menu, so Mr. Delicious there just got hired to bring them in fresh off the boat twice a week. He stays out of Old Town except for the deliveries he makes in the mornings. Otherwise, he'd be the catch of the day on every restaurant menu. He has no patience for drooling women—local or imported. But he sure does contribute to the scenery when he bends over those seafood crates."

"I will second that. Anyway, right now I need a man like I need a hole in the head," Livie added.

"Well then this will work out nicely because he's not open for business. He's pretty much a dick—always in a foul mood. I guess the universe knew that none of us could handle a man who was physically perfect *and* full of personality."

They ended the conversation to soak in the last few frames before Luke disappeared from the scene. Livie memorized the graceful way he hopped off the truck bumper and closed the tailgate for daydream fun later in the day.

BLAIR

So I went out to the Tipsy
Tortoise for karaoke after work
last night with some of the
other nurses from the office.
After seven long years, a new
Beaufort County record was set.
It took 28 songs before someone
selected "Friends in Low Places."
And I had to certify the record all
by myself. I missed you girl.

LIVIE
Fudge nuggets.

Picture it: Volunteer fireman,
pretty significant spare tire,
wearing a T-shirt that said, "I'm
a fireman, in case of emergency,
pull hose," absolutely no sense
of rhythm, could barely stand
up from all the liquor, as off-key
as I have heard anywhere, and
trying to encourage audience
participation by waving his
arms like a doofus. It was the
perfect storm.

Double fudge nuggets.

When you're the first morning visitor admitted through the guard shack gate at Fort Zachary Taylor State Park, the narrow path toward the ocean is marked just for you by electric green lizards—twirling, darting, and scampering to tell their friends that the jig is up and the humans are on the move again. If you're second or third in line at the gate, you'll miss the entire show. It turns out that lizards are a surprisingly resentful lot. Most people don't realize how long they'll hold a grudge, pouting in the brush for hours because you interfered with their plans for the day. If you're really lucky, you'll catch one dozing on a shady branch in a nearby tree. At that hour the sea and the sun get all up in each other's business and crank out a magical display that the sleepers-in will never experience. Mother Nature has a lot to say before most people rise, and Livie was taking notes during her lectures.

Real Jimmy Buffett fans lucky enough to ride the A1A hear his lyrics in everything they see, the soothing balm of his escapist message criss-crossing through each album. The masses generally associate his persona with Key West and those early days of singing in the smoky splendor of Captain Tony's Saloon. The perceptive Buffett connoisseur, though, will recognize the significance of many northerly points on the Florida Keys map, destinations like the Tavernier Hotel at Mile Marker 91 on Ramrod Key. Made famous in the song "Meet Me in Memphis" on the exceptional "Floridays" album of 1986, the Tavernier Hotel has history dating back to its construction before the hurricane of 1935. The song's speaker, struggling with the temptation to return to an estranged lover who insists her "wild days are through," considers whether or not to believe her renewed promise ("nothing replaces me next to you"), which is funny because the Keys are filled with worthwhile distractions that can easily replace just about any unfaithful companion.

*L*ivie's early morning shell collecting walks revealed to her that on any given day, the time of your life could be just around the corner. If you walk too fast down the beach, the sound of your busy feet will drown out what you were led to that place to hear. You'll miss the treasures that are all around you: peachy Queen conchs, polka-dotted Florida cones, lime green top snails, and iridescent Atlantic wing-oysters.

With her arms and pockets full of shells she'd claimed before any other pedestrians and pedalers had made it to Fort Zach's beach, Livie walked up to the rock jetty that looks across to Sunset Key in search of a picnic table. Mack was already established in a little camp, hanging from a hammock he had suspended between two trees and strumming his six-string with the earliest chords of a song he was struggling to write.

"Well, good morning, Livie Green," he sang to the emerging tune.

"Top of the morning, Mack Mason. Don't let me interrupt the musician at work."

"Regrettably, the musician is still recovering from last night's festivities. You're saving me from myself here."

"You know, one of Rita's Pain Killers will zap that hangover. You should go see her."

"I might cut bait and do that forthwith. I didn't expect to see you here so early. Looks like we're kindred spirits when it comes to the many gifts of the early beach morning."

"When you need to take stock of things, an ocean breeze can usually assist," she said.

She noticed a notepad sticking out of his bookbag in the sand underneath his hammock. It had the beginnings of a sketch taking shape that looked like it would eventually be a flamingo. Livie loved it already.

"I see you're an artist, too. Very cool."

"I'm working on a little side project—activity sheets for the unhinged and unhappy. I'm under contract with a publisher in Sarasota to produce a line of adult coloring books. We're in the drafting phase right now—my editor wants me to test the images on folks in need of therapy and collect feedback about which pictures provide the most relaxation. I would be thrilled for you to be one of my guinea pigs."

"Yes, please. I'll go buy some crayons tonight."

A few seconds of silence passed, perhaps enough time for three waves to meet their end on the sugar-white sand a few dozen feet in front of them.

"What are you looking for, Livie?" Mack asked.

The question—unexpected and pointed—rattled her into a new level of awareness. She knew he wasn't talking about seashells. It took her a few seconds of stalling to mobilize enough words to count as a complete thought.

"Well, the simple answer is that I came here to meet Jimmy Buffett. I write songs, too, one in particular I'd like for him to see. I've admired his work for years, especially his novels. I've tried everything to meet him, and it just never works out. I know it sounds ridiculous, but I came here thinking Key West would be the best place to find him."

Looking out at the ocean, Mack spoke with a flat tone that seared his message into Livie's mind. "Jimmy Buffett can't help you with what you need." He waited a second to let the impact of his statement fully land. "Put it in a sentence, professor: What are you doing here?"

The long and troublesome silence that ensued carved through Livie. She'd always been the girl with the answers. In this very off-balance moment, she had nothing. Nothing at all.

"Then I don't know," she admitted.

"Alright, then. You're on the right island to be lost. You can't sail with your anchor down. You're dragging something. Figure it out."

Livie had come to the beach that morning thinking she would find some clarity. Instead, she packed up her shells in grocery bags, hung them from the handlebars of her bike, and rolled out of the park more confused than ever. If not for Mack's parting words, she would have retreated in irritation, feeling slighted by his audacity to push on a very sore bruise. "You took the first step," he said. "You're here. Now follow through."

November 1, 2011

Dear Blair Bear,

Today the women's crapper at the Wharf clogged and overflowed, and as the newest hire, it was my job to handle the appalling situation. As I plunged and gagged, I was transported back to 1990: our eighth-grade Junior Cotillion Christmas formal. I will never forget the torment in your voice as you called to me through the crack in the master bathroom door at the home of the scandalously wealthy orthodontist whose wife volunteered their palace for the dance. As you will recall, the artichoke dip had caused a significant crisis within your bowels, and the resulting blast was more than their plumbing could handle—you know, because those rich folks must poop like sweet little rabbits. As I sailed into the loo to assess the damage and stepped around the literal shit creek that was now running through their Lifestyles of the Rich and Famous bathroom suite, I fully expected to find a silver-plated toilet plunger from Cartier beside the throne. But alas, we were stranded plunger-less because the bunny turds of the insanely well-to-do would never back up a toilet.

Those Cotillion ladies taught us how to arrange the most complicated table place settings, how to write a perfectly polite thank-you note, and how to sit appropriately with our ankles crossed and our hands resting delicately in our laps. They did nothing, however, to prepare us to handle an overflowing lavatory while wearing a taffeta evening gown and two-inch heels in someone else's house. We did the only thing we could: we got the hell out of there without as much as a word.

If we are ever in charge of the Cotillion, which I truly hope we are, we'll teach those girls what they really need to know—like how to improvise when you or one of your friends has a menstrual accident at the worst possible time or how to start the kind of rumor that will bring a cheating ex-boyfriend to his pathetic knees without word ever getting out that you were the source. Despite their champagne wishes and caviar dreams, maybe one day these girls will wind up as waitresses in a dive bar and be tasked with cleaning up a complete stranger's umps. They will need the know-how and the gastric fortitude to pull it all off without heaving. My guess is that the Junior League wouldn't be amenable to this idea, so maybe we should consider forming an Alternative Cotillion to serve the real needs of the populace. It could be our gift to the next generation of young Averites—our way of paying it forward. Have your people call my people, and let's get this on the calendar.

With Love,

Olivia June Green
Beaufort County Junior League Débutante 1994

*T*he construction of Henry Flagler's ambitious Overseas Railroad actually created Windley Key by connecting two extant islands with the material mined from local quarries. When plans for the railroad were developed at the dawn of the twentieth century, Flagler's vision (many years ahead of its time) and his sanity were probably questioned. Those who speculated that maybe Flagler's roof wasn't nailed tight were silenced in 1912 when he rolled into Key West on the first train. Dreamers just need a little bit of uninterrupted space. Give them a minute to work, and butt out.

On an overcast early Thursday afternoon in November, Rita scurried into the Wharf twenty minutes late for her shift and caught the disapproving look of Flit just three steps through the door. Before he had a chance to tear her a new one, she placed her bag behind the bar, grabbed a washrag, and began toweling off a dirty table to make herself look useful.

Watching as Flit took his stack of invoices up to the second-level "Magic Bar" to sort out the week's expenses and gripe, Rita scooted over to where Livie was refilling the fruit juice jugs.

"In the morning, I'm driving up to Windley Key State Park to go hiking," Rita said. "The weather is supposed to be perfection—not a cloud in the sky. Wear a bikini, and we'll come back looking like Hawaiian Tropic models, minus the toned abs and mile-long legs, of course. There's some kind of Parrot Head convention thing going on tomorrow, and Old Town will be a big knot of nonsense. Let's get out of here."

"Look at us—doing something outdoorsy that's good exercise and doesn't involve alcohol."

"Oh, there'll be alcohol," Rita said. "Bring a cooler."

"I've never hiked with a beer, but okay. I've also never walked out on my entire life, and look at me go," Livie laughed.

"I saw you were off tomorrow too. Flit probably made a scheduling mistake because the Wharf will be slammed. Don't let that old crab add a Friday shift on you at the last minute. We deserve a break, girlfriend."

"Hear, hear."

By the time Livie got back in the car at Windley Key to retrieve her phone (where she'd left it for the day), it was too late to get back to Old Town in time. The Facebook photos of friends and customers with their arms around Jimmy Buffett on Duval Street cut like knives. The bite was even sharper than the dozens of other times back home when similar news had crossed the wire. This had been her best chance, and she missed it. She sat in silence and deleted all the texts from folks trying to alert her to what was happening. Rita didn't know about the page of song lyrics tucked away in Livie's pocket, ragged from weeks of wear and tear. All she knew was that her friend was in the dumps for missing the chance to meet her hero.

After Rita dropped her off in the driveway of the apartment, Livie stomped up the stairs in dejection. As she unlocked the door, she heard the distinctive buzz of a seaplane overhead, a sound that would normally make her lock her eyes on the skies for a possible glimpse of the tell-tale red and yellow stripes of Buffett's seaplane, *The Hemisphere Dancer*, searching for a place to land. In her despair, she refused to even give it a glance.

Once inside, she took an obscene hunk of dark chocolate out of the pantry, grabbed her ukulele, and went out to the porch to drown herself in calories and tuneage. All of the ground she thought she'd gained in the past two months seemed lost, and she felt as wayward as she ever had in her life. Stopping only to put another gob of chocolate in her mouth, she taught herself to play "Mammas Don't Let Your Babies Grow Up To Be Cowboys," and she wallowed in the big old heap of sorry she felt for herself.

This pity party was the real deal, lasting through the night and into the next morning. She called in sick at the Wharf and spent the day pouting in her pajamas and scratching Don Ho's chin.

Then she started coloring.

"Hey, Beanee Weenee."

"Hey, Daddy."

"Mama's Christmas pageant proposal didn't get accepted by the committee at church. She spent weeks working on the blasted thing. It was an original Christmas cantata based on the history of the church to celebrate the upcoming 100th anniversary of its founding."

"Oh shoot. What theme did they pick?" Livie asked.

"Christmas in Dixie."

"Like the 1982 Alabama song?"

"That's the one."

"Whose stroke of genius was that?"

"Wanda Ballard. Well, Marty Ballard really. You know they own Ballard's BBQ, and he announced a few months ago he's running for that open North Carolina House seat. Well, they offered to donate barbeque, Hoppin' John, and hushpuppies for the whole church for a meal in the fellowship hall. Knowing Marty, he's going to use it as a campaign event. He wouldn't be able to talk to his potential constituents if we were celebrating the birth of Jesus with a joyful noise in the sanctuary. Listen, I'm fishing at Hatteras with Pete Parker, and I won't be back home until tomorrow night."

"Gracious. She's home by herself. I'll call and try to cheer her up," Livie promised.

"Christmas in Dixie is just about the dumbest idea for a church pageant I've ever heard, Mama."

"You know, people often say things were *political* when they don't like a decision, but this one literally was," Mama Green explained.

"Ever since Daddy told me, I keep envisioning the Christmas tree in the narthex covered in Confederate flags."

"Well there is always the option of holding a tractor pull there on the front lawn. To keep it in the spirit of the season, we could string them all up with imported Italian twinkle lights. I bet the Marty Ballard campaign would pay to sponsor them all," Mama said with a laugh, letting Livie know this was only a minor flesh wound.

"Maybe you could suggest a slight adjustment to the theme: Christmas in Dixie—a Redneck Holiday Extravaganza," Livie added. "They could even teach the children's choir to sing 'Grandma Got Run Over by a Reindeer.'"

"You aren't right, girl."

"Daddy told me how incredibly beautiful your cantata was. It hurts my heart that they didn't see its value too."

"Thank you, Sugar Pea. It's hard to compete against free barbeque in these parts, and Ballard's is pretty good."

"I'm fine with their sauce, but they always leave too much gristle in the meat. I don't have any patience for lazy pork pulling," Livie said.

"Smart girl. Marty's always been such a braggart about the success of his business. A few weeks ago, Daddy and I saw him with Wanda at the grocery store, and somehow

Marty got started talking about how much he had cleared in profit each year with his catering business—starting in 1988. Poor Wanda stood there with a glazed-over look like they had just run out of shrimp at the Golden Corral. The Good Book is clear on this one. Proverbs 16:18: "Pride goeth before destruction, and a haughty spirit before a fall," Mama concluded solemnly.

"Well, I've been around the sun enough times to know that you don't monkey with the Proverbs," said Livie.

"He is risen. Worthy is the Lamb."

The last tour of the Ernest Hemingway Home and Museum on Whitehead Street begins at five p.m. After the final tourists take their pictures in front of the famous $20,000-in-1937 swimming pool and buy their souvenirs in the gift shop, the property falls into delicious silence as the official gathering comes to an end. The groundskeepers make their final adjustments to the landscaping, the cats are fed, and the alarms are set.

But on some days, the party is really just beginning.

It all starts when someone neglects to lock the gate to the side entrance on Olivia Street. The sun sinks low in the sky and then disappears. One by one, the groundskeepers and a deeply trusted friend on occasion slide quickly through the gate with their brown paper bags, making sure their entrance goes unnoticed by passersby and that none of the cats escape. Everyone respects the privilege and guards its sanctity: As long as there is no commotion, their secret party location is safe.

Livie never thought in a million years that she would be sitting on Hemingway's second-story porch, her back propped against his green floor-length shutters, at midnight on a Wednesday drunk as an old coot on the bottle of rum Mack had brought to pass around.

The conversation was as deep and enjoyable as any she'd experienced in the graduate classroom. The stories got better as the night wore on and the alcohol flowed.

"It never fails," exclaimed Rick, the full-time gardener with the longest tenure on the property. "I will go out to plant a palm tree, presenting all of the context clues they would need to properly assess the situation: the potted palm tree, a labeled bag of palm tree fertilizer, a watering can. Sure as everything, a tourist will walk up in tears and inquire about which cat died."

They lounged under a blanket of stars and laughed the hearty kind of belly laughs that lowered blood pressure. The cigarette butts were carefully discarded in empty bottles, and great care was taken to ensure every aspect of the property was left just the way it was found.

By about two a.m., only Mack and Livie were left. They moved down to the patio to soak their feet in the swimming pool before locking up. With the exception of the newest litter of kittens, the rest of the descendants of Mr. Hemingway's cats (about half of which had inherited the six-toed gene) had their run of the place. It was exhilarating to see them all out at the same time—chasing bugs, playing with each other, and happily suspending their business-hours obligations to pose for the visitors' photographs and pretend to be interested in the whole scene.

"You know, I think Ernest would approve of this place being used this way: the people who really care for the property and his legacy coming in to blow it out and go nuts for a few hours," Livie said.

"Oh for sure," Mack replied. "That's the main reason we don't feel guilty doing it. Guilt is just a waste of resources anyway."

"I've thought a lot about what you asked me at the beach the other day—about who I am."

"Well, that's a good sign. Those ten years of college education worked then," he said, jabbing his elbow into her ribcage.

She took in the complete scene—the ripples in the pool made by the wiggle of their toes, the smell of some tropical flowering vine wafting on the breeze from somewhere fabulous—as she again searched for adequate words.

"I'm a little girl who didn't get the itch to go on walkabout until I was thirty-four years old. The thought never crossed my mind, and when it did, the call overwhelmed me. Instinct took over, which was a divine intervention because I would've never left otherwise."

"The discovery of paradise is a choice, Dr. Green," he said with enough conviction for Livie to believe him without hesitation. "The pace of modern life won't allow for it to fall into your lap by chance. It's life's job to knock you on your ass. It's your job to look beyond the reality of the hand you're dealt. Otherwise, you're just another cog in the miserable wheel—going round and round and round."

"Hemingway had an idea about that—the Iceberg Theory," said Livie. "He said that 'The dignity of movement of an ice-berg is due to only one-eighth of it being above water.' His idea was that the face value of things will usually suck if you aren't looking at the seven-eighths below the waterline."

"Hemingway blew his head off with a shotgun, sweetheart," Mack interjected.

Laughing, Livie said, "I know. Hear me out. He lived. He found it—before he lost it again. This house represents the most happiness he ever achieved—an ideal writing studio, a glorious tropical climate, a long road of the world's best bars, the *Pilar* docked down at the harbor, the Gulf Stream just minutes offshore, and a whole cast of Key West characters begging to be introduced into a storyline. He was doing it his way down here."

Another long pause descended—which was kind of becoming a thing when Mack and Livie talked.

Then she continued. "I felt like I was beginning to come to terms with whatever is happening to me, but missing

Buffett Friday has sucked the glaze off my doughnut. I'm just a mess. Lots of wrinkles left to iron out."

"Don't iron out anything. Happy people are the most wrinkled folks around. And ironing is stupid. Nobody likes it. Don't do it. And isn't it your guy who said 'Wrinkles only go where the smiles have been?'"

"Well, now. Somebody does like Mr. Buffett," Livie insisted, returning the nudge into Mack's ribs.

"Let's check the transcript. I never said I didn't like him. I'm familiar with his work, yes. Bigger fan of the early stuff."

"As all competent people are. Delightful, Mack Mason. Simply delightful."

"Your worries should be collecting dust on a shelf—not your dreams, Livie. Make it happen for yourself. Make it happen."

BLAIR
Ask Don Ho if he knows this one.

Did you hear about the cat who
ate a ball of yarn? She ended up
having a litter of mittens.

LIVIE
He's about to die laughing.

*9*t took her several weeks, but Livie finally convinced Flit to put livermush on the Wharf breakfast menu. A North Carolina delicacy, livermush is a cornmeal-based breakfast loaf made of pulverized pig parts, cut into slices and fried in indecent amounts of butter. It has been the go-to breakfast for generations of satisfied Carolinians. Flit was skeptical, but Livie's enthusiasm finally wore him down. He had a long-distance talk with the Neese's Liver Pudding rep, who agreed to have it shipped in small batches from the Greensboro, NC, manufacturing plant until Flit could see if it would catch on.

It didn't.

Nobody ordered it because it sounded weird. And they weren't lucky enough to have grown up in North Carolina with a Mamaw who would fry it for them on Saturday mornings and serve it on white bread with mustard.

When Livie began to hear rumblings that Flit was ready to discontinue the order, her desperation led her to do a very bad thing. She negotiated with Hector, agreeing to show him one of her boobs (he chose the left one) in exchange for his willingness to fry a big batch of livermush every morning so that Livie could put a free sample on each customer's plate and talk it up.

All it took was a little bit of marketing to help the public see the light. That and one tiny little indiscretion that nobody would ever dream of holding against her in a town like this. It turns out that the people of Key West wanted livermush. They just didn't know it.

If one is of a mind to wake up at dawn on a Key West morning, one can mosey down to Captain Tony's Saloon on Greene Street to collect the coins the really drunk tourists were too disoriented to find the night before as they tried to throw a quarter into the fish's mouth on the roof of the bar. If one is lucky, one might collect enough change to purchase a Cuban Coffee Queen café con leche, which contains enough Cuban espresso to carry your morning get-up-and-go well into the afternoon. One shot makes it clear why the Cubans are a dancing people.

A Key West bar at closing time is the playground of the folks who just want to drown it all out. Conversely, the folks who show up to a bar for breakfast and happy hour are the ones desperate to tune in. The Schooner Wharf Breakfast Club is a gathering place for thinkers and feelers, the individuals who have made the audacious decision to refuse to clock in and out on society's watch. Even so, they relish the routine and the reliability that a Wharf morning offers. They want their pancakes served with a warm smile, and Livie always had one of those to offer. The regulars cycle through like clockwork each morning. Jimbo with the silver ponytail who arrives at six a.m., sitting on the same bar stool, turning his ball cap around backwards, lighting a cigarette, ordering a Miller High Life and working the crossword puzzle in the newspaper. Tall Pat from the Sebago Watersports shack, whose job it is to hose down the docks facing the Key West Bight in the pre-dawn hours. Kristy with a "K," a waitress at Turtle Kraals who comes in for two Midori sours before her shift begins at ten.

If you've never watched a Key West sunrise from your perch on a barstool, then you've really only lived halfway.

On September 2, 1935, the Labor Day Hurricane, a Category 5 storm, decimated Islamorada, where hundreds of veterans were working on the Overseas Highway project for the US government. Almost 500 people died in the storm, many of them servicemen. When word of the cataclysmic disaster reached Key West, Hemingway loaded the Pilar with supplies and headed north to assist with the rescue and recovery efforts. The carnage he witnessed rattled him to his core. A memorial to the victims, including a crypt where many are buried, was constructed in 1937 and still stands in Islamorada.

*M*ama Green begged Livie to evacuate once the National Weather Service placed the horn of the "cone of uncertainty" squarely on Key West. When it became clear that her pleading wasn't going to work, Mama retreated to her bedroom and assumed the fetal position. Then she rallied and began trying to contact the Weather Channel for a personalized forecast of her daughter's impending doom. It was just a Category 3. The Conchs had endured much worse over the years and come out on the other side no worse for the wear. Mack told Livie that evacuations were for "liberals, tourists, and pussies" and explained that locals hunker down instead of tucking tail and running. Anyway, if you have to die, he reasoned, wouldn't you rather the papers say you were swept away from an island hurricane party by tidal surge instead of that you died from old age surrounded by family and friends?

Even so, the natives respected Mother Nature and were acutely aware of the tendency of Key West streets to flood with a run-of-the-mill summer thunderboomer, so Mack secured Livie a slot in the now fabled Hurricane Party hosted this time by Kelly's Caribbean Bar and Grill. For the past one hundred years, the locals who needed a bit of higher ground (at least a second story's worth) and a good time jockeyed for position at the invitation only get-together. Guests were selected for a wide range of potential contributions they could make to the musical, culinary, social, artistic, or intellectual climate of the event.

Mack would offer the group guitar lessons and a coloring workshop. A certified arborist would demonstrate pruning techniques most appropriate for tropical foliage. A historian from Florida Keys Community College would talk about the destruction of the fishing camp at Long Key in the Labor Day hurricane. The dancing girls from the Red Garter would lead an X-rated game of Twister and conclude with the cracking of a piñata filled with rubbers and airplane bottles. One of the rangers from Fort Zach would deliver a show-and-tell presentation about native seashells and how to identify them. A local chef would serve up a sushi-rolling tutorial. Livie's admission ticket was secured with her agreement to contribute a lecture about her doctoral dissertation, a close examination of Hemingway's use of alcohol as a trope in works like *The Old Man and the Sea* and *The Sun Also Rises*.

All invitees were encouraged to participate in a whole gamut of planned activities and games that would keep spirits bright. Fortuitously, a Jamaican calypso band in town to play the Green Parrot missed the last flight off the island before air traffic was grounded, so they brought with them enough acoustic instruments and Blue Mountain weed to ensure that the anticipated power outage would not hinder the revelry. Kelly's second-floor bar, dining room, and library would provide the perfect stage for the party once the open-air ground level became uninhabitable, and about thirty people crowded in with their sleeping bags, luggage, and pets (including five dogs, two cats, and an iguana) to await the first tropical gales.

After the evacuation mandate went into effect and the last paying dinner guests cleared the main floor, mass quantities of fish dip and conch salad had been packed on ice and taken upstairs in coolers. The pastry chef had spent the previous day baking excess loaves of coconut pineapple bread to pull the hurricane crew through the disaster. Most importantly, the bar in the upstairs lounge was stocked with enough liquor and beer to keep the crowd blissfully unaware of the treacherous emergency situation unfolding outside.

Five Key West bartenders (including Livie) volunteered to work in rotation, and even before everyone could get unpacked, the first round of hurricanes had been distributed. Always the optimist, Dottie Brackett, the manager of Hemingway's House and Museum and a pistol with a very loose trigger, passed around the "I Survived Hurricane Juana" T-shirts she'd printed for all of the guests.

In no time, the festivities were at a fever pitch, and the eclectic group of guests realized what a treat this adventure was going to be. Just as the storm began to shake the shutters, the crowd quieted for a moment. That's when a hulk-like figure wrapped in a yellow Gorton's Fisherman slicker appeared at the top of the stairs carrying a seafood crate and holding the leash of what had to be the most pitiful pooch Livie had ever seen. A gray wire-haired mutt with patches of bare skin and an unfortunate underbite, Archipelago the Dog had fallen out of the ugly tree and hit every branch on the way down.

The damp black curls that inched out of the man's hood got the attention of the most observant women in the room, but the moment was quickly forgotten as several party goers appeared on the steps behind him, returning from a quick field trip to Mallory Square, where they had gone to gawk at The Weather Channel correspondents, decked out in their foulest weather gear and doing their best to alarm the public and thus improve ratings with their demonstration of how hard it is to stand up in hurricane-force winds. The spectators had all placed side bets about how long it would take for one of the on-air meteorologists to utter the phrase "hunker down."

Mack walked up to the microphone to announce to the guests that a beer pong tournament was just about to begin in the bar downstairs, a fresh platter of fish dip had been set out in the library room, and a volunteer was needed to peel and devein twenty pounds of shrimp for dinner. Competing with beer pong and Kelly's fish dip, the request for a volunteer was met with no takers. As a first-timer, Livie knew she should step up, so she offered her services to Mack.

With a cold hurricane in one hand and his other arm around Livie's shoulders, Mack invited her to "roll up her sleeves" as he guided her to the service kitchen.

Key Largo National Guard Dispatch Officer: "Ma'am, I'm going to have to ask you once again to refrain from calling this number. Our state is at the peak of a very intense storm, and this line is reserved for emergency management personnel only."

Mama Green: "Sir, my daughter is somewhere in Key West, and she won't answer her cell phone. I'm staring an old-fashioned nervous breakdown right square in the face here."

Officer: "Again, ma'am, this is why the state's emergency management director pleaded with all residents and tourists to get to higher ground by twelve noon yesterday. There is nothing we can do from Key Largo because of the storm surge over the narrow stretches of the A1A."

Mama Green: "What is your name, young man?"

Officer: "Dillon Pendleton."

Mama Green: "Dillon, where is your Mama right now?"

Officer: "Um, she's in Apalachicola, ma'am."

Mama Green: "Well, my guess is that there couldn't be too many Pendletons in a little place like Apalachicola. I'm going to look her up and give her a call. I bet she won't be too happy that her boy is Barney Fifeing a taxpayer-funded emergency line and refusing to help a young woman in trouble or ease her poor Mama's mind for that matter. My Livie's a good girl. If you met her, you'd see why I'm so worried. Are you married, by chance?"

The dimly lit five-by-ten prep kitchen was so crammed with excess cooking equipment that there was only enough room for two people to stand. The hideous vinyl tiles on the floor and the faded and stained paint on the wall made it clear that the room hadn't had any love since Harry S. Truman relocated Washington, DC to the "Little White House" on Emma Street in the 1940s.

When Livie and Mack walked in for her to assume her shrimp preparation post, she realized how fortuitous her volunteering had been. *Maybe this is why Tiffani Triplett raises her hand all the damn time,* Livie thought.

Luke had just unpacked the last bag of pink shrimp—so fresh that they'd been swimming that very morning. They were mounded on brown paper on the stainless-steel counter in an impressive display of the bounty of the sea.

"Thanks for rounding up an assistant, Mack," Luke said. "Without help, it would be daybreak before I got through all of these."

"Sure thing, buddy. I'll come up and check on your progress in a little while. I skipped the watercolor tutorial to see the Weather Channel parody in Mallory Square, so I better make more of an effort to be participatory here," Mack said as he made his exit with a Cheshire Cat grin.

"So, I guess bringing your weight in fresh shrimp is enough to keep your invitation to this shindig open during hurricane season," Livie laughed a bit nervously. It didn't matter how attractive he was: If he didn't turn out to be a solid conversationalist, this was going to be a long row to hoe.

"I haven't found a door yet that mass quantities of local seafood wouldn't open," he said.

He's sharp. Good sign.

He retrieved two small paring knives from a small tackle box in his cooler, handing her one. Livie was reminded again of the beauty of his yummy forearms—strong, sure, and accustomed to hard work.

He continued, "I've also been asked by the host to deliver a talk about Key West pirate eradication in the 1800s for the morning program. My handouts are still in the truck."

A lecture about pirate history? This has to be some kind of cruel cosmic joke.

"You've been working at the Wharf, right?" he asked.

"Yeah, for a few months now."

"I'm sorry. I've seen you there quite a few times, but I'm never in the mood for small talk when I'm out making deliveries. It's my least favorite thing to do. *Hate* wouldn't be too strong a word. I would rather be out on my boat in the morning catching shrimp instead of having to deal with the business of selling them. Is my pissy attitude that obvious?"

"No worries. I totally get it. My dad is from Snead's Ferry, in the eastern part of North Carolina. He grew up working on the docks and sometimes on the shrimp boats. We went to Topsail Island for vacation every year when I was a kid, and he'd take me with him to go see his old friends. I've been on an ocean-going boat in the early morning hours, so I can see why you'd be sour about missing a sunrise on the water."

"Well, this all makes sense then, because I was wondering where you learned to gut a shrimp like that. I'm impressed."

"Oh, I knew how to filet a fish, shuck an oyster, and devein a shrimp by the time I was five. My Mama doesn't have sea legs, but I grew up out on the water with my Daddy."

Just then, Mack re-entered with a stack of handouts and ink pens. "Alright you two. The Boy/Girl Ice Breaker Activity has begun in the main room. Here's your homework. How are you cooking those skrimps, Luke? Do you want me to get the boiler started?"

"No, I think we just need to dust them with cajun seasoning, salt, and pepper and maybe a little squeeze of lime before we grill them. Let's use the grill downstairs while we still have power."

"Perfecto," Mack interjected. "I like a man with a dinner plan."

Alone again, Livie and Luke took turns washing their hands and writing in their answers to the questions on the handout. Their responses stoked their mutual curiosity. It had been a long time since Livie had snorted during a laugh and an even longer time since Luke had been really interested in learning more about a woman. The increasing wind speed and the now drenching rains mattered not to the merrymakers in the bar, who had officially crossed over into the land of the inebriated and very happy about it, or to the pair of young 'uns in the upstairs kitchen who were making a really good time out of peeling and deveining twenty pounds of shrimp. They had a hurricane party on, and there was no indication that it would stop anytime soon.

Hurricane Juana 2011 Hurricane Party Boy/Girl Ice Breaker

Completed by: Livie   and Luke

The Kind of Alcohol I First Got Drunk On

GIRL Rum and Coke at my uncle's fifth wedding

BOY Goldschläger — I puked golddust for 48 hours

Pet Peeves

GIRL The word "irregardless"

BOY Overbaked Cookies, men who wear socks with SANdAls

I Am A Sucker For...

GIRL Baby goats frolicking in pajamas

BOY old ugly dogs

I Have My Suspicions About...

GIRL Red landscaping mulch and any mayonnaise-based salad

BOY Shriners And their little parade cars — there's something not
right about them of a cookout

I Would Never Date A...

GIRL Polygamist

BOY mouth breather or a left-lane rider

If I Won A Million Dollars, I'd Buy A...

GIRL A first edition of The Old Man and the Sea.

BOY Nothing, I'd probably save it

Greatest Fears

GIRL the bacteria level in hot tubs and the thought of what's
in hotdogs

BOY Statues with faces

Most Prized Possessions

GIRL My Nana's china.

BOY my Atocha coin Necklace.

Next Place In America I Want To Visit For The First Time

GIRL New Orleans

BOY New Orleans

*D*runk Hide and Seek was a complete hootenanny. Each round required both the hiders and the seekers to take a shot of their choice before either counting or scrambling for cover. Drunk hiders are not necessarily covert hiders, so the rounds did not linger on, and the game and its corresponding consumption accelerated with speed, which contributed to the hilarity of the scene.

At approximately four thirty a.m., as the calypso band finished its encore and the final cocktails nudged the tipsy into their sleeping bags, the power finally went out. Livie felt around in the dark to find her bedtime things, realizing the only remaining bunking spot was beside the mayor, who was already sound asleep and snoring like a jet ski, his cell phone flashing on his belly with all of the weather alerts that were pouring into his inbox.

She got Don Ho settled in the bathroom with a litter pan, a can of food, and his cashmere pashmina bed. He looked at her with saucer-like eyes that communicated his distaste for his appalling accommodations—in the same room with two toilets, after all.

Unrolling her sleeping bag, she sensed that someone was behind her, though not in a way that startled her. "There's a much better place down the hall if you want it," Luke whispered.

Livie followed him to the manager's office to the right at the top of the stairs, where he had brought his supplies and set up two cots the day before in anticipation of one of his buddies from Duck Key joining the party.

"His wife didn't share his enthusiasm about his plan to leave her at home with three kids to attend a hurricane party in an evacuation zone," Luke said with a chuckle. "If you're uncomfortable about sleeping in here alone with me, I'll be glad to move my cot into the kitchen and sleep there," he explained.

"Oh, no need. I appreciate the offer very much. I'm an incredibly light sleeper, and I wasn't going to fare well next to Mayor McSnorington."

The office was dimly illuminated by a small emergency lantern Luke had activated. Livie's cot was nestled behind the manager's desk, while Luke's was parallel to hers on the other side. Archipelago's collar jingled as he joined Luke at the foot of the bed.

They laid there in silence for five minutes or so after Luke extinguished the lantern.

"I never asked you tonight about what brought you to town," Luke finally said.

"I was an English professor at a small college, and I just had enough of the nonsense. The majority of my time wasn't devoted to teaching anymore, and I'd turned into a professional meeting-goer. I headed south to try to figure out my next move."

"Do you have your doctorate? What's your degree in?"

"My Ph.D. is in twentieth century American Literature with minor emphases in Rhetoric and Composition and Literary and Language Theory."

"Well, that's intense."

"Ten years of college tuition just to walk away."

"What attracted you to the Wharf?" he asked.

"A steady paycheck and a view of the ocean. I'm pretty satisfied by the temporary nature of it all. Each day really feels like a new road trip that could turn on a dime into something completely different. I've never lived on the edge like that before, but I'm digging it."

"That's cool. I promise I'll be more agreeable the next time I make a delivery."

"I'm going to hold you to that now," Livie said with a grin he couldn't see.

They could hear the sheets of rain pounding the roof and the timpani echoes of the thunder as the storm cells rolled through. It was ideal sleeping weather, and they were both racked out before they realized the conversation had never really ended.

URGENT—WEATHER MESSAGE
NATIONAL WEATHER SERVICE KEY WEST FL
0355 AM EDT NOV 11, 2011
... SERIOUS DAMAGE EXPECTED...
HURRICANE JUANA ... A CATEGORY THREE HURRICANE
WITH DAMAGING WINDS, FLOODING RAINS, POSSIBLE
TORNADOS, HAIL, AND FLYING DEBRIS.
POWER OUTAGES AND FALLEN TREES WILL BE WIDESPREAD.
LOW-LYING AREAS WILL BE FLOODED.
SEEK HIGHER GROUND IMMEDIATELY.

When Livie awoke at nine thirty the next morning, the final blowing raindrops from the tail end of the hurricane tapped at the windows. Though she couldn't see him on the other side of the desk, Livie could hear Luke's slow breathing, the sign of a very satisfying rainy day snooze. She enjoyed the moment before a clap of thunderous fear resounded within her: the potential for an early morning conversation with Luke without the necessary pre-check for morning breath, dried drool dribbles, and questionable hair status. Rising as quietly as she could from her cot, she slipped out of the office. Archipelago, who had been dozing at Luke's feet, awoke long enough to raise his head and watch Livie close the door.

Don Ho was about two hours past pissed off. Nobody had bothered to feed him or tell him how beautiful he was in the morning light, and it took a few minutes for Livie to appease him. Afterward, she walked over to the breakfast buffet, which included chocolate croissants, key lime tartlets, black coffee, and mimosas. Dottie was there making a plate when Livie joined her. Despite their common interest in Hemingway, they hadn't had the chance to connect the night before.

"I'm really excited about your lecture this morning," Dottie said as she scooted two tartlets onto her plate. "It's good to have a Hemingway specialist on the island. We should talk about ways we can collaborate. I'd love to have you come and serve as a guest docent sometime."

"That sounds like so much fun. I miss the actual teaching part of my old job, and talking about Hemingway with a big group of tourists would be the best sort of fix."

Livie's presentation at ten was well-attended. She'd never offered a lecture that was accompanied by the circulation of margarita pitchers. The talk had a very different feel from teaching undergraduates—nobody was distracted by their phones (because all cell service on the island was down), and everyone was actually interested in the topic. Luke hurried into the library and took a seat just as Livie was beginning. His engagement with her talk—combined with the appeal of his slept-on curls and his sleepy eyes—was a most favorable development indeed.

After the lecture, the group had the option to take a yoga class in the downstairs bar, participate in a Cuban cigar rolling workshop in the upstairs library, or join the team that was gearing up to explore Old Town and survey the extent of the damage. Because of the risk of downed powerlines, only those guests who could pass a field sobriety test were allowed on the expedition. Not surprisingly, the search party was quite small.

Considering Luke was a man of so few words, Livie wasn't exactly sure what to expect from his pirate presentation later that morning. He launched into it with the confidence of an experienced public speaker and managed to have the whole audience invested in the story within the first few minutes. After the United States acquired Florida from Spain in 1821, Luke explained, the government had decided to maximize the natural resource of Key West's deep harbor for use as a post to fight piracy. Even though the *Golden Age of Piracy* was over (1650-1730), US officials were still concerned about the safety of American shipping vessels in the area. In February of 1823, Commodore David Porter received the commission to relocate his West Indies Squadron to fight piracy from Key West's new Naval base, launching yet another fascinating era of island history.

Luke then distributed copies of a flow chart depicting the rise and fall of the *Golden Age* and its relation to pirate activity in the Keys after 1730.

Lord have mercy, Livie thought to herself. *He isn't just a hot shrimper. He's a historian—with handouts.*

9n 1908, Flagler's railroad company established the Long Key Fishing Camp as a destination for tourists hungry for their shot at the world-class game fish that made their home in the crystal clear waters of the Florida Keys. The great western writer and pioneer sport fisherman Zane Grey used the Long Key community as his base of operations for many seasons in the days before the hobby of big-game fishing had transitioned to sport. The Long Key camp was obliterated by the 1935 storm, but the spirit of those earliest anglers could never be squelched by a hurricane. The ocean's great gifts are tempered by her dangers, and the generations with sea water in their veins never lose sight of that risk.

"Oh my Jesus Lord, child. Why in the world haven't you answered your phone?"

Mama Green's conniption was authentic, and she needed Livie to know it just as soon as possible.

"I've called everyone I know to call looking for you—hospitals and morgues as far up as Miami, the incredibly unhelpful National Guard. I even contacted the consulate in Cuba in case you got washed off the end of America and floated down there on a piece of debris. All I could think about was the possibility of you being intercepted on the beach by Fidel Castro and me and Daddy having to pull Barack Obama off the golf course to try to get you freed up. Turns out we don't even have an embassy down there—a bunch of Swiss people with unintelligible accents are running it. It's just a long dad-blamed story."

"Take a deep breath, Mama. And a nerve pill. I lost cell service the night of the storm, and then everybody's phones went dead once the power went out. I was just fine the whole time."

"I can't do this, Olivia. You are going to have to work with me here."

"I know," Livie said in the most reassuring voice she could muster. "I'm perfectly safe, and I love y'all. I promise—no more hurricanes. I'll evacuate next time."

"Well you better, because Carter is all jacked up about riding one out now, and I can't lose two babies that way."

"Carter doesn't have sense enough to come in out of the rain, much less a hurricane," Livie said.

"It's not the time for jokes, Miss Priss."

"Yes, ma'am."

Three days after the storm, order (at least the relative kind that could be achieved in Key West) was beginning to be restored. The airport had reopened, the Old Town streets were cleared of tree limbs, and the cruise ship dock was once again populated by the gargantuan floating turds of the sea and thousands of tourists yearning to soak up as much culture as they could in a fraction of an afternoon. Passengers raced down the gang plank, bought Key lime pies on sticks, and boarded the Conch Train, where they would hang their heads out the window like dogs trying to take pictures of the lighthouse, the Audubon House, and the Southernmost Point, which the tour guides always failed to point out was just a painted sewer head cover. Then they returned to the ship in self-congratulation (their overpriced T-shirts in tow) for having *done the Florida Keys*.

When Livie arrived to work at her usual time, she was disappointed to see that Flit was filling in for Rita, who had gone up to Miami to visit a cousin. There weren't many benefits to sharing part of a shift with Flit. He was an ornery old grouser whose humor had been knocked out of him in the boxing ring decades ago. On the bright side, he did know his Schooner Wharf history, and he would often insert his knowledge into discussions with a staff member who was being reprimanded for not doing a particular aspect of the assigned job correctly.

When Flit learned that someone had forgotten to move all of the ketchup bottles from the tables into the refrigerator before the hurricane, the whole bar got a lesson out of it.

"We have to take pride in what we have here—one of the most historically significant bars in a town full of historically significant bars. Details matter. We are the bar of Mel Fisher, the greatest treasure hunter of all time. For years he sat on these very bar stools with a rum and Coke and conducted the business that led to the discovery of $400 million in treasure just a few miles from here. His crews used to dock their salvage boats a few slips down the way. We're the Schooner Wharf, people. Let's act like it."

This wasn't the first Livie had heard of the legend of Mr. Fisher, and it certainly wouldn't be the last.

Around eight, with Flit still barking about inefficiency and work ethic, Livie took the initiative to retrieve a crate of clean beer mugs from the kitchen before they were actually needed. She was lugging the glasses to the bar when she met Luke, toting his own crate full of fresh shrimp. He was an extra special pretty in the morning, and Livie saluted whoever came up with that idea.

"Good morning, sunshine," she said with exaggerated enthusiasm.

"So, I've had my coffee (with a shot of Kahlúa), and I'm prepared to be both personable and conversational this morning to make up for my less-than-sociable behavior during my previous deliveries."

"Well butter my butt and call me a biscuit."

"Where do you get these phrases?"

"It's one of the many gifts of growing up in the Tar Heel State."

Looking down at the cooler, Luke said, "Make sure Hector doesn't overcook these. They are perfect, and it would be a crime if their preparation didn't match their pedigree."

"I'll look after them for you. Might even make a shrimp BLT out of them at lunch."

"That would be a very good call. You hold it down in here," he said.

The Key West roosters have to be the happiest birds who ever did live, and they are not shy in telling you about it. Each morning they *COCKADOODLEDOO* about all they witnessed the day before, narrating their storylines in a macho call and response that reverberates across the island. Even after several months of living in Old Town, Livie still felt compelled to say *Good morning* to every puffy-chested feathered friend she met on the street and to offer *You don't says* and *I didn't know thats* in reply to their stories. It was just the right thing to do.

*A*fter finishing up another epic set at the Wharf (and this time having a crowd that truly appreciated his talent), Mack came over to settle up for the month with Flit and get a beer from Livie.

"We had a jumper at Hemingway House yesterday," he added, while Flit grumbled and wrote the check.

"Oh, how awful," Livie said, pouring the PBR from the tap.

"No! He jumped in the pool. It was hilarious. It happens about twice a year. If you pay attention, you can spot the people who are about to do it. Yesterday's chap took off his flip flops and unloaded his phone and wallet from his pockets over by the cat drinking fountain. He took a running start, dove into the shallow end, and smacked his dense head on the bottom, possibly knocking some sense into it (but it's too early to tell). It tears Dottie up every time. She cussed him up one side and down the other as he was being escorted off the property and permanently trespassed."

"See, this is precisely why I moved here. The last interesting thing that happened at my university job was the day a sociology professor walked past a freshly painted wall in the administration building that was clearly marked with a 'DO NOT TOUCH—WET PAINT' sign. He couldn't help himself. His big handprint is still visible there in the hallway, and all the professors joke about it. That story is always good for a laugh at a faculty meeting—because we are a sad lot of emotionally constipated people."

"Sounds like your colleagues would benefit from a field trip to … anywhere really."

"Testify."

BLAIR
Last night a group of church
choir members came through
to spread some holiday caroling
cheer. When I leaned down to
ask one of my elderly patients
which song she'd like to hear,
she told me to go to hell.

LIVIE
Doesn't the Bible say, "Blessed are
the nurses who don't smother their
patients with their own pillows for
they will inherit the kingdom of God?"

Yep. It's in the book of
Paul I think.

Oh, and tell your deviant brother
thanks for the Christmas card.
I didn't realize he was still
defrauding the US Postal Service
by refusing to use stamps and
addressing the cards to himself.

Just waiting for them to find him
out and bring him to justice.

*T*he men who busted their humps to complete the Overseas Highway in the Sunshine State's oppressive heat and humidity did so without the conveniences that make Florida Keys life such a relaxing escape for modern-day travelers. It is said that once they reached the stretch of the project that is now Marathon Key, they remarked among themselves how much a pain this "marathon" of a job was becoming. The name stuck. For people moving down the map from Key Largo to Key West like pilgrims honoring the stations of the cross, Marathon is the halfway point of the journey toward the Promised Land. Just fifty-nine more little green signs to go.

The coiffure of Mama's life was impeccably styled, except for one extremely wild hair—her NASCAR obsession. While the Green household revolved around the Father, the Son, and the Holy Ghost, Dale Earnhardt, Sr. had always run a very close second behind the Trinity on Daytona 500 day. The whole family was allowed to play hooky from church because if Preacher Wayne got long-winded, they might find themselves perilously close to missing the most important green flag of the season. Mama would rise before dawn to line her driveway with enormous checkered flags. Using all of the strength in her 5'1" frame, she would slide her life-sized replica of Earnhardt's iconic No. 3 car out onto the front lawn to sit prominently throughout the day's festivities.

Her homage to the Intimidator for the past ten years had sadly turned into a memorial after the terrible accident in the fourth turn on February 18, 2001. Mama just about lost her marbles in her grief, keeping the giant plywood car in front of her house for a solid two months afterward in tribute. Of course, the neighbors all thought the spectacle was tacky as hell, but they kept their mouths shut for one simple reason: Mama kept their mouths full of the world's best homemade peanut brittle at Christmastime, and they would all rather crawl naked across a bed of broken glass than piss her off and risk being unceremoniously removed from the delivery list.

This was to be the first yuletide in more than twenty years that the peanut brittle would not be delivered exactly one week before Christmas Eve. Mama and Daddy loaded up "The Beast," their new forty-foot monstrosity of a motorhome, and headed south to spend the days before Christmas 2011 with Baby Girl. Mama was skeptical about passing a winter holiday in a tropical climate, but she sure was glad to have a bonafide excuse to miss the Christmas in Dixie debacle. Daddy's fervor for the Beast's maiden voyage and Carter's willingness to participate in an abbreviated leg of the trip (flying down to meet them for a weekend) won her over. After two days on the road, they picked up Carter at the Islamorada Airport and continued south to their destination: the Jolly Roger RV Park in Marathon. After a weekend with the kids, Mama and Daddy would linger for a few days in the middle Keys before returning home.

On her way back down the Keys from Miami, Rita volunteered to stop at the Jolly Roger and pick up Mama, Daddy, and Carter for the drive into Key West. They weren't sure they'd be able to find a place to dock their house on wheels in Truman Annex.

Mama squawked like a chicken when she saw Emma Street, exclaiming that it looked like a scene right out of Beverly Hills. Then she hooted and hollered about the beauty of Livie's apartment. You'd have thought she was touring the Biltmore House or somesuch. She squeezed Livie's neck again and again like it had been years separating them instead of a few months. Livie was happy to indulge. It felt good to have her Mama there.

After hugs and kisses, Daddy set to work replacing burned-out light bulbs, repairing a leaky faucet in the bathroom, and changing the water filter in the refrigerator. It's what Southern daddies do.

Carter called dibs on Livie's couch, and Livie worked out a reduced rate from the property management company for one of the empty units in Mills Place for Mama and Daddy. Everybody had a place to lay their head. With only a weekend all together, Livie wanted to make sure everybody got to do exactly what they wanted with their time. Key West had absorbed the energy of one Green, but it was going to be interesting to see how four of them would be tolerated.

"Me and the guys finally pulled the perfect prank on Davie Rawlings," Carter said, opening another Landshark on Livie's balcony.

"Y'all have to stop this before someone gets hurt," she said. "Seriously."

"Poppycock. After they stole my truck and made me drive that short school bus around for a week, I realized it was my calling to up the ante and show them how the game was played."

"Bunch of hooligans. That's what," Livie said with an odd mix of disgust and desire to hear more.

"A few weeks ago, Johnny Ballard got his dose. We threw a fully-clothed tackling dummy off an overpass right in front of his car. It was funny as all get out."

"Carter."

"But back to Davie. You know those beautiful old hardwood trees in his front yard?"

"Uh huh."

"Well, we waited for him to leave for the beach last weekend, and we cut them all down. Ronnie McCall brought over his boss's stump grinder and a few rolls of sod. You can't even see where those trees used to be."

$\mathcal{I}$t had been way too long since she'd wet a fishing line with her Daddy. Honestly, this was all he wanted out of the trip—a few hours alone with Livie. They went down to the White Street Pier while Carter and Mama explored Old Town on foot. He was proud that he'd raised a daughter who could take her own fish off the hook.

"I've tried to explain it to your Mama," he said after the first grouper splashed into their bucket. "Your brains, your beauty, your gumption—you got all of that from her. But your need to be near the water came from me. You sure did choose a pretty place to live, honey."

"Seeing this slice of ocean every day has been very good for my soul, though I'm sorry my change of plans caught you so off guard."

"As long as you and Carter both find contentment, I can go to my grave settled. The same is true of Mama, though she could stand to behave a bit better about it. This time away from that gossipy prayer group will do her good. She needs to get out of the stew for a while. All of the husbands—Dwight Rawlings, Pete Parker, Lyman Triplett—are tired of getting caught up in the hullabaloo, which is why we all play golf twice a week. Not a one of us is any good at it, and we don't even particularly like it, but it gets us out of the house and away from the insanity. Listen, I lose sleep at night thinking about you working in a place where bouncers are necessary, and I sure do miss seeing you every day, but I completely understand what you're doing. Take your time, Sweet Pickle. There's no rush."

The tug on Daddy's line was another exquisite dinner table fish. He wondered what side dishes they'd pair with their catch for dinner tonight at the apartment. Livie wondered how any girl could ever make it through life without a Daddy.

After a dinner of grilled grouper and pineapple risotto, the Greens walked down to the Mallory Square Sunset Festival, an event that was without argument the quintessential Key West experience. The buzz of the charged crowd filing in from a dozen side streets combined to form a palpable concentration of human energy and anticipation. Daddy immediately fell in with a sword swallower/fire twirler and couldn't pull himself away. Mama, Carter, and Livie pushed on through the sea of humanity past a patriotic contortionist and a chicken that had been trained to walk backwards to the beat of Michael Jackson's "Billie Jean."

Then Mama made stern eye contact with a fortune teller, who rose from his cardboard table to tell her that his pack of Tarot cards had important things to teach her about her future. She wasted no time rebuking him in the name of Jesus—out loud—and praying for the cleansing and deliverance of any festival-goers who might have been sucked into his sorcery. Sensing a brewing confrontation, a small pack of onlookers began to assemble, at which point Mama began quoting spiritual warfare scriptures verbatim and shining the light of the Lord on the dark arts. It only took fifteen minutes or so for them to all have church right there in the middle of Mallory Square, with the befuddled psychic (who really should have seen it coming) trying to figure out how his show had been taken hostage. Mama used the tips she accrued to buy the whole family Conch fritters, which they ate happily with their legs hanging over the dock as the sun took its last big breath and exhaled the day.

Judging by the pounding of the hangover hammers on Livie's forehead when she rolled over in bed, there weren't words to describe how hard she and Carter had hit Old Town the night before. As she figured out how to make her legs work again, she heard a disconcerting rattle and felt something cold and hard up against her leg. As her panic increased, Don Ho came alive with the clattering of whatever had them, and in a tangle of sheets, they both spilled off the bed with a painful thud.

Two hand-painted maracas that Livie had never seen before lay exposed on the empty mattress.

She crawled down the hall, grateful that Mama and Daddy were safely sequestered a few apartments away from the disappointing scene, one that proved without dispute that she and her brother had turned into the people their parents had warned them about. As Livie struggled to steady her hand and scoop the espresso into the French press, she looked out the window and located her derelict brother, passed out in a lawn chair wearing nothing but a beach towel around his waist and an ornate sombrero on his head.

The scene conjured up flashes of memory her brain had somehow backed up and saved. *A conga line on the sidewalk in front of the Smallest Bar in the World. Carter in a tattoo chair getting a nautical compass emblazoned on the back of his shoulder blade. A whole cluster of tequila shots on the counter at the Lazy Gecko.*

Just the thought of tequila made Livie acutely aware of her dry mouth and her desire to heave. Then the frantic full-body search for tattoos commenced.

With three minutes left before the coffee was brewed, she fumbled for her phone, which turned out to be the storehouse of information that would refresh her memory the rest of the way. *A picture of Livie planting an unwelcomed kiss on Flit's cheek behind the Wharf bar. A candid of a shirtless but not yet sombrero-ed Carter playing the tambourine on stage behind Mack at the Lazy Gecko. A group portrait at the Southernmost Point of Livie, Carter, and a delegation of Japanese businessmen wearing matching "I Heart Key West" tank tops over their company's polo shirts. A snap of Carter beside the Shell Man statue wearing nothing but the sombrero and the tat and mercifully facing toward the Shell Warehouse.*

It was the *Key West Morning After*. And it hurt.

After pounding a bottle of water and two Tylenol, Livie was off with Mama Green to delight their palates with one of the island's many well-kept secrets: Sarabeth's lemon ricotta pancakes. Mama had been informed that there would be no grits on the menu, and she promised not to question the chef's decision on the matter. Considering how much Mama loved breakfast, Livie knew Sarabeth's would be a hit.

"You know," Mama said, "Tiffani Triplett is going to be down here in a few months on her cruise. It would be nice if you gave her a tour around the island and showed her where you live."

"You can give her my phone number if you want to, but I suspect she feels the same way I do. I'd rather sit for a surprise root canal than take her anywhere. The only thing we have in common is the place we grew up. Let's change the subject. What else is happening back home?"

"Fair enough. Well, Carter has a new girlfriend that we really like."

"Does she realize he's serious when he says he's never getting married?"

"I hope so."

Livie was convinced that Carter's good looks would never fade, nor would his irresistible appeal to women. He would be perpetually attractive and never under any pressure whatsoever in Avery to get married. That burden would fall instead on the long line of women who dated him. They would be in charge of dodging the nosey questions and making all of the excuses at the weddings and baby showers of their friends.

"And I think there is a whale of a mess brewing over the Silver Queen Corn Festival this summer," Mama continued. "One of the newly elected town council members is fixing to get creative with the program to try to draw in folks from a wider geographical radius. There has been quite a hubbub about it in the letters to the editor of the paper."

The conversation made Livie miss that part of Avery— the constant tug of war between tradition and change and how a few thousand people who dearly loved their little town handled it all.

"I don't have a good feeling about it, but we'll see what the council decides," Mama said. "I'm so glad we came down here. I can't wait to tell everyone how beautiful your neighborhood is and how pretty you look with that tan. I'll always be proud of you, Olivia, even if I'm not quite sure what you're doing. And before we leave, I have to see if the waitress will give me the recipe for this pancake batter. It's so good I'm thinking about smacking *my* Mama."

"Hey, don't look now," Livie whispered, "but there's a girl at the table behind you with a giant ring pierced through the middle of her nose."

"Let there be peace in the valley," Mama said with genuine concern once she turned around for a gander. "If she doesn't need a touch from the Lord, I don't know who does. She looks exactly like one of those Hereford bulls Uncle Merritt used to raise in Dallas. I bet her Mama is mortified. That's even worse than Carter's new tattoo."

"Now how do you know about that already?" Livie asked, absolutely stunned.

"Olivia, I know everything there is to know about my babies. Once you are a Mama, you'll understand. Until then, don't doubt me."

"Yes, ma'am. Never did. Never will."

BLAIR
Happy New Year! Last night,
a Jeep Wrangler pulled up to
the ER foyer, and two guys
dumped their buddy out without
stopping completely. Poor guy
had balls swelled to the size of
grapefruits. His journey back
to consciousness was a painful
one indeed. He awoke with no
recollection of the events that
precipitated his regrettable
injury. We think alcohol may
have been a factor.

LIVIE
Oh my Jesus Lord.

You don't even want to know
what we had to do to get the
swelling to go down.

Boys are so dumb.

There were big doings on the island, and of course, it all started with a tourist. Dottie was in the Hemingway House bookstore that January 2012 morning when an impressively large woman bounded through the door with a Kleenex wrapped around a scratched and barely bleeding finger. "Holy Moses, I've been mauled," she shrieked. "That stupid cat mutilated my hand. I want to speak to the manager. Immediately!"

The cat in question—Jane Mason—was anything but stupid. In actuality, her IQ was probably a few ticks higher than that of Nancy Schneider, a mammoth sunburnt Idahoan tourist who was now barreling into a full-blown hissy right there in front of the Ernest Hemingway refrigerator magnet display.

"I'm the manager," Dottie calmly inserted. "Let's get you in the back here and put some Neosporin and a bandage on it."

"I assure you I need more than mere first aid for this wound. Where is the closest emergency room? How long will it take an ambulance to get here?"

You would have thought Jesus was calling Nancy Schneider home.

While the medics loaded the hysterical woman into the back of the ambulance, Dottie and Mack worked to retrieve the surveillance footage from the security cameras around Hemingway's writing studio where the alleged assault went down. Despite the profuse signage around the property warning visitors to avoid feeding, petting, or holding the cats, the video revealed that Nancy Schneider had first lured Jane Mason with a grilled shrimp that was stowed away in the grocery bag she was using as her purse that day because there was rain in the forecast and she didn't want to risk ruining her new Dooney and Bourke cross-body pocketbook freshly shipped from the Home Shopping Network. After the shrimp, Jane Mason was lulled with the chin scratches afforded by Nancy Schneider's talon-like press-on fingernails. The third stage of the plan—to capture a picture for Facebook of Nancy Schneider holding Jane Mason—is where things went cattywampus.

Nancy's husband, the hapless Hal Schneider, surprised Jane Mason from behind, scooping her up as quickly as he could and shoving her into the waiting Pillsbury dough arms of Nancy, who was already smiling like a mule eating briars for her close up. Jane Mason, none too pleased by the tomfoolery of the Schneiders from Idaho, let out a warning cry that alerted everyone outside on the museum's property that she was unhappy. Unwilling to relent until a flattering photo was taken, Nancy Schneider increased her grip on Jane Mason, which is when the claw of the kicking back foot of the cat lightly scraped the index finger of her captor.

After the ambulance pulled away and the crowd dispersed, Dottie said a little prayer that the whole matter would be settled once the drama queen was laughed out of the ER.

The next morning as Dottie was opening the property for what was sure to be a busy day—with three cruise ships set to dock—she heard her office telephone ringing. "Good day. This is Preston Biggerstaff, Esquire, of Biggerstaff, Biggerstaff, and Bickers in Miami. I am calling on behalf of my client, Mrs. Nancy Schneider. She wanted me to inform you that litigation was filed this morning in the Monroe County District Court. The Ernest Hemingway Home and Museum has been named as the defendant in the civil case pertaining to the heinous assault that she endured from one of your cats yesterday."

"Well, isn't this charming?" Dottie said sarcastically. "Might I ask what Mrs. Schneider is requesting as compensation for her injuries, which, as I recall, necessitated a squirt of Neosporin and one of the smallest bandages in the box?"

"She is seeking $1.5 million in damages to cover the ambulance ride, the ER visit, her anticipated plastic surgery needs to repair what turned out to be significant damage to her index finger, PTSD counseling, and, of course, pain and suffering. Ms. Brackett, did you know that Mrs. Schneider is a piano teacher in Meridian, Idaho—one of the best in the business? She fears that her mental anguish will prevent her from ever playing the piano again. Oh, and we filed a Dangerous Animal Report with the Monroe County Animal Control Office this morning as well to request that the savage and possibly rabid animal be immediately quarantined and hopefully euthanized."

Before the Animal Control officers could load up and come to question Dottie, she'd already called Livie, who dashed over with a pet taxi to whisk Jane Mason away to the safety of her Mills Place apartment. Don Ho was delighted to have company, even though his new roomie wasn't excited about being kept inside. Dottie signed the officers' affidavit, swearing that Jane Mason had run away immediately after the incident and had not been seen since. By afternoon, word about the lawsuit was on the street, and by sunset, "Save Jane Mason" banners began appearing on front porches all over town.

Dottie turned over the surveillance video to the Hemingway House's lawyer, who assured her that nothing would come of the claim if it reached trial because any logical juror would side with the cat, especially after seeing evidence of the twenty-three warning signs on the property. Biggerstaff, Biggerstaff, and Bickers would not relent, sending Dottie threatening letters almost daily. On the day of the trial, a whole legion of Florida Keys SPCA protesters gathered outside the courthouse to await the verdict and sling fake animal blood on Nancy and Preston as they exited if necessary. As Dottie and her lawyer left her office for the hearing, they were met at the door by Nancy Schneider (in a full cast up to her elbow) and Preston Biggerstaff (in what had to be a $1,000 suit).

"We are here to extend an olive branch and to try one more time to reach an amicable settlement before trial," the lawyer explained. "Mrs. Schneider is willing to accept an even $1 million dollars as compensation for her injuries and her losses. You should recognize the courage it took for her to come back to the scene of the crime today, especially considering that the wild beast is still on the loose and unaccounted for."

"I have an even better idea," Dottie seethed. "Mr. Biggerstaff, I suggest you take your olive branch, slide it into your client's greedy asshole, and pull it out nice and fast."

"We will see you in court," the Hemingway lawyer added with a zing, doing his best not to crack up.

You can call it the providential hand of the Lord or mere coincidence, but what happened next shocked even the most hardened citizens of Key West.

Conch Telel

February 2, 2012

Conch Train Tragedy

Nancy Schneider of Meridian, Idaho, was killed Wednesday after she stepped off the curb on Whitehead Street in the direct path of a Conch Train. Mrs. Schneider, who was in town with her lawyer, Preston Biggerstaff, to settle a legal claim against the Hemingway House for an alleged injury suffered at the paws of one of its six-toed cats, was apparently distracted by a coconut milk vendor on the way to court and did not check for oncoming traffic in her excitement to join the line. Key West Police confirm the Conch Train driver was not at fault in the accident, and no charges will be filed

That evening, the Karma Party (as it was being billed) at the Hemingway House still took place under cover of night, but the guest list expanded dramatically to include the entire staff, with Dottie setting up a full mix-it-yourself bar under the awning outside the bookstore.

Livie arrived quite a bit late with the guest of honor. Riding in Don Ho's cat carrier, Jane Mason made her triumphant return to the property. About half of the party's guests were already three sheets to the wind, and because she had to work the next morning, Livie knew she would make no attempt to catch up to them.

"Well if it isn't the Queen of the Duval Crawl," Mack laughed, putting a very cold beer in Livie's hand. "You know that Navy cadet never in a million years thought he would lose that bet for his sombrero with you. I think twelve shots and walking out under your own power is some kind of record at the Gecko. And Carter is an exceptional tambourine player. Tell him my offer still stands for those gigs as a duo."

Livie buried her face in her hands, knowing there would be many more embarrassing moments of atonement like this one to endure in the coming days. She was happy when the conversation turned and Dottie asked her to regale the crowd with a Hemingway story fit for the occasion.

Livie chose the day in 1936 when Hemingway and the poet Wallace Stevens got into a fistfight on Waddell Avenue.

"Wally had been caught talking trash about Ernest's sister," Livie began, "and Ernest went downtown to settle the score. Interestingly enough, Stevens at the time was perhaps most famous for 'The Idea of Order at Key West,' a thinking man's poem that explores the philosophical question of what happens when imagination and reality meet. Well, forget imagination and reality. When Hemingway and Stevens met, the scuffle resulted in the novelist knocking the poet into a muddy puddle. Envision it—two of the greatest minds of the twentieth century beating the snot out of each other on the streets of Key West."

As Livie was concluding the story, Luke walked through the Olivia Street gate carrying a platter of congratulatory shrimp with cocktail sauce. He gave Dottie a big bear hug and echoed the sentiments of all in attendance: *right always wins in the end.* When Jane Mason wrapped her tail around Luke's leg, begging for a shrimp, Mack reminded her that shrimp was what got them into this whole mess to begin with.

"I'm afraid I can't stay," Luke explained. "The weather is going to finally cooperate tomorrow, so I'll be out in the boat before the sun comes up. Enjoy the shrimp, guys, and have a few cold ones for me."

On his way out, he gave Livie's ponytail a playful tug.

As midnight approached, most of the staff members had made their way—fully clothed—into the swimming pool. They exited when needed in their sagging clothes to get another drink or pop a few shrimp.

Before Livie excused herself from the festivities, Dottie thanked her one more time for hiding Jane Mason and keeping it top secret until the whole saga concluded.

"As far as we're concerned, you're part of the staff now," Dottie said. "If you ever need anything at all, we'll be here."

Livie then had a moment of realization. Though Key West seemed very far away from North Carolina, she'd really never left the South, where neighbors help neighbors and friends are family.

The waitressing lifestyle is full of occupational hazards. Therefore, it's only fitting that some perks are involved too. When you work at a tropical ocean-front bar, every now and then a waterspout will drop out of a squall line and ignite the crowd. When you celebrate the little things, even more of them seem to come your way.

BROTHER
Are you aware of what our
mother is doing to telemarketers
these days?

LIVIE
No, but I have to know now.

I was over there today for lunch.
Daddy was helping me change
the alternator in my truck. The
phone rang, and she picked up
in the laundry room. I only
heard her part.

"Oh, I have been praying for
the Lord to send me someone
to witness to, and hallelujah,
my plea has been heard in
the heavenlies. Tell me, do
you know Jesus Christ as
your personal savior?"

HAHAHAHA! Get 'em, Mama!

And she was completely sincere.
God love her.

"I've enjoyed talking to you, Sugar Booger, but I absolutely have to go. There's a mutiny brewing on the Missions Committee at the church," Mama explained. "Betty Varner insisted that we adopt an international theme for last week's Valentine's Day fundraiser. Despite our vigorous protests, nothing would do her. We all fumbled around in our kitchens for weeks trying to learn how to make empañadas, lo mein, and matzah balls. Carol Rawlings even tried to make Korean kimchi. Poor thing fermented that God-awful stuff in a bucket in the garage until Dwight couldn't take the stench anymore and threw it out in the woods. It was just the worst hodgepodge of a buffet any group of Baptist women has ever pulled together. There we stood with our sad ethnic dishes when Queen Betty waltzed in with two of her famous Sun Drop pound cakes, which of course turned out to be the only edible things in the fellowship hall. As she basked in the glory of having her cakes disappear within minutes, the old biddy even had the nerve to lie—in the house of God no less—and say she got the recipe from a French cookbook, you know, because of all that Sun Drop they drink in Paris. The worst part is that she told Eunice Turner beforehand that it would be nice if the cooks dressed up in a costume that represented the cultural heritage of their food. Ninety-three-year-old Eunice showed up dressed like a Viking and carrying a dish of some sort of undercooked salted fish. Mary Grace Parker is angling to have Betty's chairmanship revoked, especially for humiliating sweet Eunice in what have to be her final days. Everybody who didn't get a piece of Betty's Parisian pound cake left hungry, and they all congregated at the Cracker Barrel in Hickory Grove to eat breakfast for supper and talk about her behind her back. She's not worth the white part of chicken poop, and I don't know of a Christian way to handle her. Word is that Preacher Wayne is going to call us all into his office after service on Sunday to cover it in prayer. It's all just a hot steaming mess."

*E*ven though she had pushed academia away, Key West had managed to lure Livie back into side conversations with the authors and literary texts that had sustained her through the rigorous doctoral process. As she stopped her bike on Caroline Street in the minutes just before the rays of the sun began snooping through the feathered palm fronds like peeping Toms, she looked up at the Jessie Porter House and thought about Robert Frost. The poet had lived in the cottage out back for sixteen straight winters. Her mind turned to "Birches," her favorite Frost poem because of its dichotomies and dualities—the sharp edge of reality (an ice storm bent the tree branches) moderated by the speaker's urge to imagine a different scenario (maybe those branches were bent by a carefree boy at play). Though published in 1916, long before Frost came to Old Town, Livie could see through this text what had attracted the writer to the island. Key West has a tidal sensibility—a simultaneous push and pull that very much mirrors Frost's poetic unwillingness to land on either side of a wavering scale. The moment of ambiguity was much more interesting to him than the finality of any answer. Life happens in the in-between.

*L*ivie had lately become addicted to the house salads at Kelly's Caribbean Bar and Grill. The citrus vinaigrette did a rumba with the cashews, the sliced strawberries tangoed with the goat cheese, and the fresh bed of tender greens was the ideal dance floor. On the evenings when Mack would play a night set, she would walk three blocks from her apartment to listen to him and commune with her salad.

His normally sedate program in the second-floor bar of the mostly dignified restaurant had turned into a riot as a women's softball team on their last night on the island had passed the entire happy hour from four to seven scarfing as many half-priced drinks as they could hold down.

The result was a very vocal and invested audience whose antics devolved from PG fun to Rated R debauchery by the time nine rolled around. Mack handled the uproarious scene like a pro, and Livie nearly choked on her salad a few times.

"I'm convinced that we must find little ways to be deviant every day but still keep it between the lines so nobody notices," Mack said when he joined Livie at the bar. "This is the key to a happy life, as the fine young ladies in the audience tonight clearly demonstrated," he added.

"Well, they have the deviant part all worked out," Livie insisted. "And after six months of living here, I can say without reservation that the happy part has found me, too. It's weird. I've never been more unsure of the future, but I've never felt better. One thing is certain: I needed to live in a place where Cuban rice and beans were at the ready any time of day."

"Amen and amen. Still no sign of Mr. Buffett, though."

"Nope. I go down to Margaritaville once or twice a week. The people watching pulls me through a few overpriced drinks. Missing him a few months ago provided some necessary perspective."

"I saw Luke throwing a little flirt your way the other night."

"I doubt it was a flirt."

"I've known Luke for a few years now. I can assure you—that was a flirt."

"Maybe, but I doubt it. For the record, I'd be a fool to ever object to cozying up to him in any capacity. I totally didn't see that historical lecture about Key West piracy coming at the hurricane party. I get the sense that there are a lot of mysteries waiting to unfold with him."

"Oh, yes," Mack nodded.

"I don't think he has any interest in dating, though, at least not if you believe all the women who have crashed and burned trying to catch his eye."

"He's mature beyond his years for a variety of reasons most people don't understand," Mack explained. "He can also assess the potential drama of any situation—or woman—with laser precision, and he doesn't have any use for it. Once you are his friend, you can always count on him. I know the same will be true when he decides to let himself fall in love. He's a good kid—like you. I'm rooting for both of you."

Livie dropped a twenty-dollar bill on the bar to pay both tabs and kissed him softly on the cheek.

"You are good people, Mack Mason."

On the first Wednesday night of every month, a most important Key West cultural moment transpires at the Green Parrot Bar on Whitehead Street: Two hundred or so locals file in with their instruments for the group sing-along that is Ukulele Night. Even uke beginners are welcomed into the fold. Once Livie heard about the plan of several bartenders to perform "No Woman, No Cry" together at the March gathering, she practiced the necessary chords for weeks to make sure she was ready. By the time they reached the bridge of the song, the whole crowd was in perfect unity. The repetition of the chorus, one that Livie had heard hundreds of times before without as much as a thought, now poured over her in revival: *Everything's gonna be alright*....

It was just a regular old Friday in late April down at the Wharf. With a small crowd of contented customers gathered around the main bar, Livie took a break to sit and feed some leftover toast from an abandoned plate to the Mama chicken and six little puff-of-fluff chicks that had wobbled in from the street. Rita was rolling silverware in napkins to get ready for the lunch rush and keeping the patrons occupied in conversation.

Livie heard the old over-worked engine of Luke's Ford rumble to a stop out front.

Maybe Mack was right, Livie thought. *What if pulling my ponytail was as much of a flirt as Luke would concede?*

Luke smiled big as he carried his crate over to the kitchen, his herculean effort to seem amiable in the morning on obvious display. After Hector signed the invoice, Luke propped his empty crate up next to the bar, ordered an orange juice in a to-go cup from Rita and sat down at the table where Livie was feeding the family of now very friendly chickens. The humidity had prompted little beads of sweat to form below Luke's hairline, and Livie had to fight the urge to touch them inappropriately.

He got right to the point. "I have an idea to run by you. Next weekend, the Mel Fisher Museum is hosting its annual gala at the Casa Marina. It's a legendary party. I have two tickets because I'm on the board of directors. It's a costume ball, but I have all of that figured out if you don't object to falling in with a bunch of treasure hunters and passing a drunken night with them."

"You had me at Casa Marina," Livie said. "I can't wait."

"Perfect. I live in the Stock Island Lobster Company yard about ten minutes from here. If you don't mind coming out, I'll have your costume ready, and we can take a taxi in from there."

"And what are our costumes?"

"Oh, I could tell you, but then I'd have to kill you, and that would defeat the purpose of inviting you. This contest is cutthroat, so our identities are classified until the night of the party."

"Sir, yes sir," Livie said with a salute.

"Well, these shrimp aren't getting any younger, so I'm going to move on down the line."

"See you on the flip side, Shrimper Dan."

"Funny. And I get it," he quipped.

"I knew you would, which is one of the main reasons why I'm going to the Mel Fisher Museum gala with you."

As Luke toted his crate back to the truck, Rita, the unapologetic eavesdropper who was now breathless from shock, darted over to Livie.

"You know there are women in this town who are going to put a hit on you now. They will try to kill you and make it look like an accident. This will not go unnoticed. I'd watch my back if I were you."

"Rita. Girl. It's just one date. And it might not even be a date. He probably just didn't want the extra ticket to go to waste."

Even as she played it all off with Rita, Livie couldn't ignore her growing excitement. The truth was that she hadn't stopped thinking about Luke since the hurricane party. He was a book she was itching to open, and her patience with unopened books usually didn't hold out very long.

It had been a long time since Livie had crammed. She needed to know everything there was to know about Mel Fisher and his sixteen-year quest to find the 1622 wreck of the Spanish galleon *Nuestra Señora de Atocha*. The ship, packed to the gills with treasure and headed back to Spain from the New World, had left Havana's harbor under perfect skies on September fourth. A vicious fall hurricane consumed the ship and several other vessels in the twenty-eight ship convoy two days later, just thirty-five miles to the west of Key West. Amazingly, the Spanish had diving capability in the 1600s, and with the mizzenmast of the ship jutting out of the water, they were able to locate the *Atocha's* remains and retrieve a tiny fraction of her holdings. A second hurricane just a month after the first one wiped away any evidence of her watery grave, setting up a 350-year mystery that required the smarts and perseverance of Mel Fisher to crack.

Livie was consumed with the story in the days leading up to the party. In fact, she spent the morning and afternoon of the gala dilly-dallying in the Mills Place swimming pool and plowing through Eugene Lyons' fabulous *Search for the Atocha*. The next piece of the Luke puzzle had been revealed: He was a Mel Fisher Museum board member. Livie, who usually prided herself on being among the first to arrive at the solution to any conundrum, was stumped. But totally intrigued.

Because the taxi driver didn't want to get tangled up trying to find a turnaround spot in the Stock Island Lobster yard, he dropped Livie off at the Oceanside Marina entrance. As she crossed the road to enter the fenced lot, she noticed the Maloney Street road sign. *I wonder if Walter C. Maloney had anything to do with that?*

she thought, smiling to herself at the interconnectedness that seemed to hold the fabric of Key West life—both past and present—together.

Luke's house provided the perfect explanation for his personality. His bungalow stood among the lots owned by dozens of individual lobster companies. On any given day, the lobstermen would be out painting the buoys for their lines and preparing the wooden traps for their next trip to the ocean floor. Six hundred square feet divided among two very humble weather-beaten stories was all the house Luke needed. The teak-wood shack was surrounded on all sides by wrap-around porches filled with rocking chairs and hammock swings, making it possible to find a comfortable perch to enjoy an approaching thunderstorm from any direction. The backyard abutted the marina and offered the dock space he needed for his trawler, the *Anne Bonney*, named after the famous female pirate from Ireland who disguised her identity so she would be accepted at sea. Luke's commute to work was as long as his sidewalk. It was the ideal hideaway for a bachelor who made his living on the ocean: A bedroom and bathroom upstairs and a downstairs kitchenette, powder room and living room—complete with two shelves full of books about nautical lore, pirates, shipwrecks, underwater archaeology, and marine fisheries.

Livie was greeted on the porch by the barking howls of Archipelago. He gladly laid down at Livie's feet, exposed his pot belly and waited for an obligatory tummy rub. Hearing the commotion, Luke came out already costumed, his embroidered cloak with its standing ruffle collar making him the stuff of a seventeenth-century señorita's most randy dreams. Adding in the trunk hose, knee-high leather boots and feathered tri-corner hat pushed it all right over the edge.

"So, has my security clearance finally been approved?" she asked as Luke welcomed her through the door. "The suspense is going to do me in."

Laughing, Luke unzipped an enormous garment bag, revealing an ornate green silk cinched-waist gown. The high collar built into the back of the dress made way for a plunge in the front of the neckline that would show the tiniest peak of strategic cleavage. Livie could tell even without trying it on that her boobs were going to look good in it.

"We are Martín and Doña María Salgado, two nobles who were returning to Spain aboard the *Atocha* in 1622 after Martín served for years as the secretary of the court in Lima. The extravagance of the 300 pounds of silver that we claimed on the *Atocha*'s manifest was rivaled only by the treasures we stuffed in your dressing trunk as contraband to avoid taxes."

"Oh Martín, I had no idea you were such a renegade."

"Well, Peruvian court life will do that to a fellow. You can use the bathroom behind you to get dressed if you'd like."

Immediately regretting what all those Casa Marina banana coladas had done to her waistline back in September, Livie began to pray out loud: *Jesus, I need to lose ten pounds in the next sixty seconds or so. Your word says that through you all things are possible.*

She sucked in. She twisted. She shimmied. Then she discovered the Lord's remedy for her predicament: a row of buttons built into the boning of the bodice that allowed her to release the few extra centimeters of material that would make it possible for her to wiggle into the gown. *Glory to God in the highest.*

Luke was waiting outside, holding the final component of their costumes: the heaviest lengths of gold chain she'd ever seen—one set for his necklace and another for her belt. The costume store had outdone itself on these outfits.

"Thank you, kind sir," Livie said demurely with a curtsey.

"Of course, my dear," Luke responded with a regal bow.

On the way out to meet the taxi, Livie again noticed the Maloney Street sign.

"Hey, do you know if this road is named for Walter C. Maloney?" she asked. "I read his Key West history the night before I came down here, and I loved everything about it. In fact, I realize now that the book was the impetus that caused me to get in the car the next day and leave my job."

Luke didn't say anything for a few seconds, long enough for Livie to fret about whether she had somehow said the wrong thing.

"It is in fact. He was my great-great-great-great-great grandfather. I can't believe you read his book."

Now it was Livie's turn to have no words. None. At. All.

They stood there for a few beats in their regalia, looking at each other and trying to wrap their heads around the coincidence.

"So, you are a Maloney then?"

"Sort of. Lucas Maloney Spottswood."

The bust of Florida State Senator John Maloney Spottswood stands proudly in the Key West Sculpture Garden facing the sea. Born in Key West in 1920, he was also the Sheriff of Monroe County in the 1950s and 60s. At the time of his death in 1975, he was the largest property owner in the city, his holdings including the La Concha Hotel and the Casa Marina. Senator Spottswood, in addition to being Luke's grandfather, was also descended from Alexander Spotswood (spelled with one "T" in those days), the Colonial Governor of Virginia famous for pulling the strings that led to Blackbeard's ultimate demise. Under contract with Spotswood to track down the notorious (and totally awesome) pirate, Lieutenant Robert Maynard made good on his charge in 1718, killing Blackbeard at the Battle of Ocracoke Inlet—just a hop, skip, and a jump across the Pamlico River from where Livie was born and raised. The family line also included Walter Cathcart Maloney, the writer of *A Sketch of the History of Key West, Florida* and one of the city's first mayors. It was on July 4, 1876, that Maloney stood to recite his newly written compilation of Key West's history, an oratory that was later published in book form. It's doubtful that as he delivered his speech, with the sound of the celebratory firecrackers popping behind him, he realized his words would change the life trajectory of one of his descendants 135 years later.

It's difficult to adequately describe the extravagance of the Mel Fisher Division Week Gala. The architecture of the grand lobby of the Casa Marina lit up for a party was too beautiful to pass without stopping in reverence. The round archways of the enormous windows and the dark, warm finish of the hardwood floors and paneled ceilings carried Livie back to the 1930s. She could easily imagine Hemingway gliding through the main door for lunch, a rich caramel tan on his exquisitely toned legs and the tropical sweat causing his linen shirt to cling with lust to the contours of his back.

The main party was set up on the Casa's scrumptious little strip of beach and around the dazzling pool, the very one where Livie had been privileged to loaf for an entire week. The extravagance of the table settings, the floral arrangements filled with Birds of Paradise and elephant ears, the food, and the band was beyond compare. The theme was "Shipwrecked," and predictably, the soirée was filled to the brim with slutty mermaids, *Gilligan's Island* characters, and Titanic crew members. Luke and Livie raised their first drinks to commend the originality of their costumes and their prospects for winning top prize in the contest: a $2,400 silver coin recovered from the *Atocha* wreck, a miles-long site that was still being actively excavated by Mel Fisher's family despite his death in 1998.

Livie quickly scanned the informational signs posted around the party's perimeter to get a sense of where she had landed. "Division Week" is a week-long celebration for the Mel Fisher Museum's investors. After buying shares in the company's finds for a period of 365 days, the financial backers gather to collect on their division of the treasure. In the Museum's main offices, investors make private appointments to take possession of their cash, gold bars, silver coins, emeralds, pottery, and other artifacts. The party was packed with treasure hunters, marine archaeologists, wealthy investors, and everyday people willing to cough up a hundred thousand dollars to inject some needed adventure into their lives.

Luke and Livie had just had time to procure a second round of Coronas from the bar when the locals began to take notice of Luke's presence—with a date. Mrs. Gertrude Simonton, an exquisite woman of eighty who was, of course, dressed as Mrs. Howell, cornered Luke.

"Your grandfathers would be so thrilled that you are still involved in the affairs of the city and the success of the museum. Have you thought any more about running for mayor, dear?"

"Oh, no ma'am. I'm too busy right now with the shrimping business to think about politics."

"Well, keep it on your radar, young man. We could use another Spottswood in office—someone who knows our history and has seen first-hand the detrimental effects growth has had on our little town."

Then out of a sea of slutty mermaids emerged what was apparently the madame of them all. Francesca DuPont, a well-known realtor in Old Town, had opted for the borderline pornographic Golden Glimmer "Working the Street Corner" Mermaid costume, her painfully obvious fake breasts suspended by two woefully inadequate gold lamé seashells. Her golden fishtail (which fit tight like a cheap condom) was covered in the most distasteful black fishnet ever conceived by a Beijing manufacturer. She was a strikingly beautiful woman with long, thick brown hair and even longer trim legs—a good seven inches longer than Livie's. In moments like this, it really sucked to be 5'2".

Years of living in the rural South had made it possible for Livie to spot a pageant girl at one hundred paces, and she was certain that this tramp had a "Little Miss Something" sash tucked away in the back of her closet somewhere.

Interrupting sweet Mrs. Howell/Simonton mid-sentence, Francesca slithered her arm through Luke's on the opposite side from where Livie stood.

"Well, if it isn't Luke Spottswood, looking dashing as ever," she purred. "When are you coming to my office for that lunch we've been trying to schedule? We need to get together to figure out how to take the museum board to the next level."

Reclaiming his arm as politely as possible from her grasp, Luke moved toward Livie and placed his hand on the small of her back. *Score one for the North Carolina girl.*

"Oh, Frannie," Luke said. "I really don't think the direction of the board should be decided in a closed-door meeting by fewer than half of the members. Maybe we need to call Kim, Charlie, and Bruce and schedule a day-long planning session to outline some new goals and priorities."

"Not to change the subject," she said, changing the subject, "but I found our senior prom pictures when I was doing some cleaning the other day. Can you believe I dried the corsage you gave me, and I actually still have it in a box somewhere? That was a *very special* night. Do you remember going out on Garrett Baker's family's boat afterwards? We were so drunk …."

"This is Livie Green, by the way," Luke said, putting a stop to the unsolicited trip down Memory Lane. "She's new in town and working at the Wharf."

"Well isn't that adorable," Francesca managed to utter with a lack of sincerity a woman could detect but most men would be oblivious to. "I can't fathom the riffraff you have to deal with at a place like that. It must be terrible," she insisted before dissolving into a cackle.

Rita wasn't kidding.

"Oh I try to avoid talking about my clients outside the office to protect their confidentiality," Livie said, only half joking. "However, I did manage to sift through the Wharf rabble and find a good-looking shrimper to bring me to this fine party tonight, so I can't complain."

"Touché," Luke said, impressed.

"Well, Luke, I will have my assistant give you a call and at least book a lunch so we can catch up. It's been way too long," Francesca added as she walked away, but not before reaching out to give his forearm another squeeze.

Livie knew this girl would eventually require some handling, but she hoped she would be able to do it with subtlety.

Once the sun was down, the fun of the party really began. Luke and Livie sat in a ring of Adirondack chairs surrounding a stone fire pit. The roaming bartenders kept a cold drink in every hand, and the stories that flowed about the treasure and the years-long hunt for it were more fabulous than Livie could even process in the moment. One person in the circle was a current conservator on one of the salvage ships, and two others were divers at the Marquesas site on July 20, 1985, the day the *Atocha* Motherlode was discovered.

What Livie had read about in Lyon's book just that afternoon was springing to life right in front of her, and she could barely contain her curiosity and excitement. She was enthralled and too busy to notice Luke sitting back in his chair and reveling in the fact that all of this registered with her. With each excited question that she asked of the group, Luke found it harder and harder to take his eyes off of her.

It was excruciating to pull herself away from such unbelievable conversation, but three Coronas had made it necessary for her to shake the dew off her lily.

As she finished her business, she heard the door open and another customer enter the bathroom. The razor sharp click of the stilettos caused Livie to pause just in time to see the slow saunter of a gold lamé mermaid tail under the crack of the stall door.

Well damn. This is how it ends. She's going to kill me in the bathroom.

Francesca didn't even look away from the mirror where she was applying additional black eyeliner when Livie emerged.

"I dated him for over a year. He was my first love, and our breakup was a terrible mistake," Francesca said.

Livie knew better than to respond to a manipulator at work.

Instead of taking the bait, she went in search of Corona number four. And a crowd of witnesses just in case.

LIVIE

I'm on a date with that cutie patootie shrimper
I told you about, so I can't talk, but if I turn up
dead or missing tomorrow, have the police
investigate Francesca "Frannie" DuPont.

BLAIR

10-4, good buddy. Are you
okay with me sharing our little
text exchange here with the
producers of your episode of
"America's Most Wanted" when
that time comes?

Sure, as long as you promise to
get a skinny actress to play my
part in the crime re-enactment scenes.

Livie found the closest bar, but Francesca was hot on her trail.

"I think maybe we've gotten off on the wrong foot here," Francesca said curtly. "Let me give you some advice that I think will help you navigate this town more effectively. I have known Luke my whole life, and there is a long line of women like me who have patiently waited their turn for him. You can't just waltz into town, put on a smutty bar maid's T-shirt, and jump the line. He's been distant for the last few months, and I see now that your interference is the cause. Beyond that, the city needs him to continue the legacy established by his family over so many generations of public service here. We won't allow some fly-by-night waitress to mess that up."

It was such low-hanging fruit. It would have been a crime to leave it on the vine.

"That's a *post hoc, ergo propter hoc* fallacy."

"Pardon me?" Francesca asked, now completely on tilt.

"*Post hoc, ergo propter hoc*—it's Latin for 'after this, therefore resulting from it.' It's a fallacy used by speakers and writers who don't know what the hell they're doing. Here's your logic: *Livie got here. Now Luke doesn't seem interested. Therefore, Livie pulled Luke away.* See how that doesn't square? I'm not your problem. Leave me out of it."

"Well, I have never."

"Clearly. And you need to rethink your logic in the unfortunate event that we should ever have to interact with one another in the future. Just in case, I have a book you can borrow that will probably get you caught up enough to be able to follow along."

As Francesca retreated to the nearest dark corner to find a rock to crawl under, Luke, who had been watching and listening from a safe distance, moved in behind Livie, wrapping the ironwork of his forearms around her waist and pulling her close, back to belly. Leaning down to reach her ear, he said in a low voice, "You just unpacked her lunch and ate it in front of her. There will never be a way for me to express how much I enjoyed that."

In all Livie's days of taking breath on this earth, nothing had ever felt better than this incredible moment of being close to him. The smell of a man who worked hard on the salty sea in counterpoint to the unexpected sweetness of his coconut aftershave created a dissonance that drove her into pheromonal overdrive. It was official: She was a goner.

It was as surreal as a Key West moment could be: Luke and Livie ascending the emcee's stage arm in arm as seventeenth-century Spanish aristocrats, and Luke accepting the *Atocha* coin for first prize, bowing like a true nobleman to his love, placing the coin in the palm of her trembling hand and then gently kissing her knuckles.

Holy crap on a cracker.

The taxi waited by the curb for the return trip to Stock Island while Luke and Livie savored their last few moments as the Salgados.

"Really. I can't keep this coin," Livie insisted. "You paid for the tickets, and you came up with the brilliant costume idea and rented the clothes. All I did was show up and drink a case of Coronas."

Luke put his hand over his gold *Atocha* coin. "I have one. You have none. End of discussion. I want you to have it."

Her *I don't even know how to begin to thank you* speech was interrupted by the most sensational, serendipitous kiss. Its simplicity—no technique or tongue—called every nerve ending in Livie's body to full attention.

"I can swing by tomorrow afternoon and pick up your dress to get it back to the costume store," he said, concentrating on his words to make sure he made sense after the fabulous kiss concluded. "Maybe we could get lunch somewhere."

"Better idea: How about I cook lunch, and we take a picnic out to Fort Zach?"

"Deal. I do, however, need to take the gold chains back tonight so they can go to bed in the safe."

Livie focused on her balance to prevent her knees from buckling under her.

"Why would they need to go in a safe? They're from the costume store on Roosevelt."

"Not quite. They're from the *Atocha*, brought up in '85 with the Motherlode."

When she left the Casa Marina, Livie had been reasonably sure that her bladder would be capable of holding that last beer until she got home. Now she was reasonably sure that she was going to piss herself right there on the doorstep.

"I thought I told you," he said not very convincingly. "Good thing you didn't lose it, right?!"

Oh no, I'll be losing it—on the other side of this door in a few seconds.

*L*ivie's phone rang at seven thirty a.m. It could only be
Avery, and Livie prayed nobody was dead.

"What's wrong?" Livie exclaimed (louder than she
intended) into the receiver.

"Nothing's wrong—well almost nothing," Mama
quipped. "What are you still doing in bed? Are you sick?
Are you pregnant?"

"No, I went to a museum gala last night and was out late."

"I sat next to Mary Grace Parker last night at the
Rotary auction. Tiffani Triplett just got back from her
cruise. While she was in port in Key West one night, she
walked by that *bar* where you work and saw you inside,
sporting a pair of those Spandex underwear Hooters girls
wear and no bra under your tank top. She said you were
serving buckets of beer to a bunch of dirty fishermen who
were ogling over you."

"Oh, mother. Please hear me. I work the morning shift.
Secondly, my breasts are entirely too large to go without
a bra—even around the house. And nobody in Key West
wants to see my buttocks hanging out of the bottom of
Lycra Daisy Dukes. Why do you continue to worry about
what she says?"

"I'm beginning to wonder if she might have it out for
you, Livie."

"You think, Mama?"

"And I'm worried that people will believe her."

"Hey, I have some news that I think will take care of that
worry. I was invited to that museum gala by a wonderful

man. He's a shrimper down here—I think Daddy would really like him. It's very early, so don't go booking the country club for a wedding reception or anything."

"Jesus, Mary, and Joseph. Oh. Murphy, get in here! Livie's got a new boyfriend. Oh. Does he come from good stock? Murphy get in here! Oh."

"Very good people, Mama. You can't even imagine."

"What's his name?"

"Luke."

"Luke," she said with approval. "I like that. I like that a lot."

After the phone call, Livie laid in the bed and rubbed Don Ho's ears while she processed all that had happened the night before. Then she remembered that Luke would be coming in just a few hours, expecting the lunch she promised.

Like any Carolina girl worth her salt, Livie's cooking was her ace in the hole, a card only played when one was reasonably sure a man was a keeper. In fact, generations of Southern women had made the strategic decision to go to bed with men before they revealed their cooking prowess. It just wouldn't be right to get their hopes up if it wasn't going to work out in the end.

Livie didn't hold back a thing as she scurried around her kitchen and made it happen just the way her Mama, Nana, and Mamaw had taught her: she fried chicken with a honey pecan glaze, she mashed potatoes with a profane glug of heavy cream, she baked buttermilk biscuits to be served with orange marmalade, she drowned corn on the cob in lime butter, she chopped cabbage for Baptist cole slaw, she stirred a jug of sweet tea, and (the pièce de résistance)—she frosted Mamaw's trusty brownies. The night before, she had kissed the man of her dreams, and this was no time to play around.

Even though the skies were ominous when Livie and Luke loaded the picnic basket in his truck, they decided to take their chances and go to Fort Zach anyway. Livie had worn her favorite jungle green bikini—the one that provided the slight lift and tuck that she needed—under a fetching tropical kaftan she had found on clearance in a boutique on Front Street.

She recognized Mack's bike on the rack as they unloaded the food, beach chairs, fishing rods, and tackle box.

"Look at that," Mack said from the comfort of his hammock. "Key West's most eligible bachelor and bachelorette together at last. The rest of the folks here don't realize it, but that storm is going to stay out to sea. I bet in a few minutes you two will have the park all to yourselves."

"Please join us," Livie begged. "I made enough food to feed a whole regiment."

"I appreciate it, but I'm playing the Smokin' Tuna's happy hour at four, and the tip jar tends to fill more quickly when I've showered. I was just about to pack up. I'll leave my hammock here for you, though. Livie, you can bring it down to the Wharf tomorrow, and I'll pick it up after my set."

"We appreciate that," Luke said, extending his hand and helping Mack extricate himself from the hammock. After depositing a quick kiss on Livie's cheek and delivering a knowing glance that only she could see, Mack strapped his guitar to his back and pedaled away.

Luke promptly discarded his T-shirt, revealing how much good shrimping actually does for a body. Livie had never dated a man who piloted his own sea-going vessel. She was clearly making better decisions these days. In kind, she stripped off her kaftan and began unloading the Tupperware dishes on the picnic table. As Luke set up the beach chairs, he was studying her from behind with great interest.

Once the buffet was opened, Luke ate—and he ate ugly—temporarily losing his manners and approaching his plate with reckless abandon. It had clearly been some time since this boy had been offered a home-cooked meal.

Southern Girl - 2, Realtor Bitch - 0.

After lunch, the fullness of his belly pooched out from its normally flat frame. *Fat as a tick* was the appropriate descriptor. Livie could tell he was going to be in some level of pain later.

"I don't know what just happened," he said as he pushed his plate back, only partly kidding. "I'm dizzy."

"You just threw down on a meal prepared by a good Christian woman of the South. At the end of your life, this will likely be recorded as one of your better days."

He laughed but then cut it short when he realized how much it hurt.

"Do you mind if I ask you a really personal question?" he said, turning serious.

"I'm an open book. Shoot."

"What's a girl as smart as you doing slinging drinks at the Wharf?"

"I don't exactly know yet. Maybe for the same reasons that a man like you is more than contented catching shrimp when the whole town would apparently vote for him to be mayor. The simple answer is that girls in my hometown are groomed to meet expectations, of which there are many. I was one of the best at hitting all the marks (except for the marriage part), but I was the most unhappy about it. I woke up one morning—after reading your great-grandfather's book actually—and realized I had been clapping off rhythm to the song of my own life. Everyone on the outside looking in didn't see it. Deep down, though, I knew I needed to find the beat to be happy. For the first time, I'm starting to hear it. Something is happening, and until I know what it is, I'm parking it at the Wharf. Does that make any sense at all?"

Luke stared out at the foreboding but harmless storm. "Oh, yeah. You just explained my life from age sixteen to the present. Say no more. I get it. I come from a very long line of successful lawyers and politicians. Taking to the sea on a shrimp boat in what was then a dying industry and enrolling in Florida Keys Community College to take business courses instead of hopping on the law school hamster wheel was not at all what my family had in mind.

"At the peak of the Lower Keys' shrimping boon back in the '50s and '60s, there were several hundred trawlers going out of Key West. But in the 1980s, Asian shrimp farms took off. They were and are still stuffing those babies with every chemical agent and dye under the sun and selling them for pennies on the dollar compared to American shrimp. Regulations have also discouraged most entrepreneurs from investing in the industry. I'm one of the last handful who have stuck around, mainly because I'm happy with a modest living. There's a growing number of restaurants and fish markets that are willing to pay a premium to bring their customers local shrimp harvested in unpolluted waters. It took a lot of legwork for me to find them, though. I'm banking on the movement for clean food to grow, and I think the Keys shrimping industry will rebound with it. I'd love to own a whole fleet of boats someday, but I'm doing just fine. And if my prediction is on target, when the market comes back around, I'll already be established with enough vendor relationships to capitalize. None of this was an easy sell to my dad twenty years ago, though."

"Now my turn," Livie said, steering the conversation back to the night before. "Will you tell me the story of those gold chains?"

"It's a tale worth telling. My dad was an original investor when Mel Fisher came to town in 1969 in search of the 1622 galleons. When I was around five I remember visiting Mel's houseboat on Roosevelt and going with my dad to the Chart Room to talk to Mel about the recovery prospects. I would beg my dad on weekends to take me to the *Golden Doubloon,* Mel's floating office/museum at the Key West dock. I remember when it sank in the 1980s and going down to see the spectacle, its stern completely submerged in the bight and most of the starboard side leaning into the water. In a town full of loonies, everyone thought Mel was crazy and that my dad was even crazier for giving him even a nickel of the family money. But through all of the court cases, the years of financial losses and tragedies, the bad press and the failed leads on the Motherlode, my dad always believed in Mel.

"After my mom died of cancer when I was three, my dad really lived vicariously through Mel's adventure, and that couldn't help but rub off on a kid like me. By the age of eight or nine, I had set up a nautical radio in my bedroom to monitor all of the boat traffic in the area. I heard the call the day in 1985 when the Motherlode was found, and I phoned my dad about to explode with excitement. It was a Saturday, and he was working on a big case, but he promised we would head out bright and early the next day to find out where they were.

"It took hours to get out to the Marquesas on Sunday— the longest hours of my life. By the time we arrived, there must have been a hundred small boats docked around the salvage ships. The only way to get on board was to hop from boat to boat, but we made it over in time to see the two thrones of silver bars erected on the main deck. A few minutes later, Mel sat atop one throne, drinking champagne out of a plastic cup, and Jimmy Buffett sat atop another, playing his guitar and joking with the crowd. Buffett was a good friend of Mel's, and he got out to the discovery site as soon as he heard what was happening.

"It was pure magic, especially seeing those relics before they had even been cleaned. I was only eleven, but I was out of school for the summer, so my dad and I stayed well into the night. That's probably the best memory I have of my dad. We got those two gold chains in the very first investors' division that took place in 1985. They are worth a small fortune, but my dad always took them out of the safe when I wanted to see them. I inherited them when he died five years ago. Heart attack."

"Do you have any brothers and sisters?" Livie asked delicately.

"No, but I have tons of aunts, uncles, and cousins scattered all over Florida—a lot of them in the Lower Keys."

The cloud cover would likely prevent any sunset show later, but the only two remaining beachcombers in the park didn't care. They fished wordlessly on the jetty rocks—side by side—shooting each other knowing looks each time one of them caught a fish that stood as the biggest one so far. Luke fought off the urge to take her down right there on the rocks when he realized she knew how to bait her own hook.

The sparks from the night before hadn't been false positives. There was no need to put into language what was happening between them. They both just allowed themselves to be folded into the batter of whatever cake the Good Lord was whipping up.

After a few hours of fishing and a steady decrease in the number of bites due to the outgoing tide, Luke looked back at Mack's hammock gently swaying in the breeze beneath the palm trees.

"After all that lunch, I could sure go for a hammock nap. I wonder if it fits two," he said.

"Only one way to find out."

Luke scooted in first on his back, forming the perfect little curl against his body for Livie to roll into. He tucked one arm around her and rested his other arm behind his curls. *There it was again: the salty musk and the coconut aftershave.*

"Oh, God," he said, looking out at the whitecaps on the ocean. "I'm going to need an actual reason to compel me to ever leave this spot."

"For my third-grade North Carolina history project, I wrote a stellar report about Blackbeard's manner of death at the Battle of Ocracoke Inlet." She didn't know why she was telling this story, but her mouth started moving before she could come up with a strategy to stop it. "Then I made this super-cool panorama that explored all of the legends about what happened to his dismembered head. I probably read ten books way outside of my grade level to put that project together. My teacher—Mrs. Grainger—gave me a C- and wrote on my essay that 'it is unbecoming for a little girl your age to write about such a gruesome thing. Your poor topic choice is the sole reason for your lowered grade.'

"When my Daddy got home from work and saw her comments on my paper, he went down to the school and lit her up like she had stuck her finger in a hot socket. He told her that while the other girls in the class were researching no-brainer topics like Native American basket-weaving, I had the courage and intelligence to think outside the box. She should be ashamed, he told her, for attempting to stifle the imagination of a creative child."

"I like your Dad already."

"He's just the best one ever."

"You know what I can't figure out?" he asked. "How all of this book reading about my ancestors landed you in this hammock with me."

No answers were necessary, so they leaned into the comfort of the silence. They were gently awakened two hours later by the sprinkles of rain that announced the shower that had finally decided to come inland. Mother Nature held off just long enough for the island to fully cast its spell.

MURPHY GREEN
Is this Olivia J. Green?

LIVIE
Daddy? Are you texting?

It went through! Look at that.

It did. Welcome to the twenty-first century.
We're glad you could make it.

Your Mama told me you were
seeing a new fella. I'm not there
to look this boy in the eye, but
Carter thinks I can monitor the
situation from back home by
texting. You let that young man
know that I just disassembled
and cleaned my pistols, and
they're all in good working order.

Yes sir, I will.

Okay then. That's all I've got.

ONE LITTLE SHRIMP
LONELY AND BLUE
ANOTHER IN THE NET
SHRIMP MAKES TWO

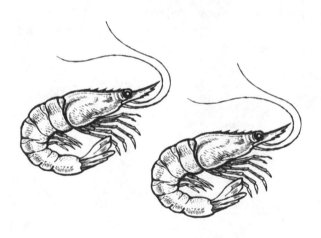

*L*uke didn't understand it. At all. Why Livie would be willing to waste a perfectly sunny Saturday in June to drive three hours north to Homestead to the closest Krispy Kreme doughnut store was a mystery to him. "There's a donut store on Roosevelt," he reminded her. Preferring not to utter the name aloud, Livie explained (yet again) that The Big D, while serving donuts that closely resembled doughnuts in both name and appearance, was the worst sort of imposter, baking sad replicas in a dark manufacturing plant in Boston and then FREEZING THEM (Lord help us) before shipping, defrosting, and distributing them to the unsuspecting public.

"Once we get to Homestead," she said, "you'll understand."

So they drove behind the long, slow caravan of campers and minivans full of retreating vacationers heading back to reality on the mainland, and Luke tried to wrap his head around the need for the trip.

They arrived in the Krispy Kreme parking lot to find that the red sign in the window was not lit, sending the signal to the faithful that the appointed time was not yet upon them. "We can go inside and buy a box anyway," he said. "No, we wait," she said. "Trust me on this one."

After half an hour on standby and after watching approximately twenty cars successfully navigate the drive-thru, it happened. The warm red glow of the "Hot Now" sign alerted all that the time was nigh. The tiny rings of fresh, delicate dough had begun their journey down the assembly line toward culinary perfection. As the freshly baked morsels emerged from the hot oven, they headed toward the crescendo of their evolution: the cascade of glaze that would help them transcend their little earthly bodies and enter the heavenly realm. They were conceived—Livie was sure as baby rabbits of it—by the Divine Creator to secure the happiness of mankind in this life and beyond.

"I will take a dozen hot ones," she said with authority at the counter.

"We'll never eat a dozen," he said with an alarming degree of doubt.

"That dozen is for me. I would recommend that you order similarly to avoid certain regret," she said.

As Luke's full lips wrapped around that pivotal first bite at their table, it all came into focus—the years of calories wasted on *donuts* from quick stops, mediocre bakeries, and (ashamedly now) The Big D. With a flake of warm glaze on his chin and a twinkle in his eye that can only come from that virgin sugar rush, he was ready to return to Key West to preach the good news about the transcendental experience available to all a mere three hours north.

On the drive home, Luke, who was now wearing the distinctive KK paper hat to demonstrate his allegiance, noticed Livie's tanned feet bouncing to the beat of the songs on his scratchy truck radio, the light pink of her toenail polish making her tiny nails look like delicate seashells on some Caribbean beach. He liked it all. Her feet on the dash. Her quirks and kooky ideas spilling over into the planning of his weekend days. The syrupy sweet aroma of the peppermint oil she rubbed on her temples to ward off headaches, the same oil that he sometimes smelled from the bottle she left on the end table in his living room. He had failed to notice when it all actually came together, but the balance they had achieved put him at ease.

As they were zipping across the Seven Mile Bridge, Livie was overwhelmed by the need to tell Luke the truth.

"One of the reasons I came down here was to try to meet Jimmy Buffett in a bar during a surprise visit. A few years back, I wrote a song I wanted him to see. I thought that was my goal, which seems foolish now. Mack told me a few months ago that the reason I was really supposed to come here actually had nothing to do with Buffett. I didn't see it then, but he was right."

Luke reached across the seat and grabbed her hand. She was hoping that he wouldn't let go, and he didn't.

BLAIR

Good news. I got that job at the family practice I applied for. No more nights and weekends in the ER!

LIVIE
Well, shit the bed.
Congrats, Blair Bear!
When do you start?

I put in my two-week notice at the hospital today, and I don't start the new position for three weeks. Do you happen to have a couch I could crash on for a few days?! My legs are pasty white, and I fear I've forgotten how to have fun.

Get on down here, girlie! And see if you can smuggle a few Cheerwines in your luggage. I fear I've forgotten what they taste like.

I'm on it, sister. The TSA won't be the wiser.

Our disorderly Southern reunion caused quite a kerfuffle in Key West's little speck of an airport. Even though it was only nine thirty a.m., Livie was already pounding a Cheerwine as we walked arm in arm to the parking lot.

"This humidity ain't no joke," I said. "It's hotter than a four-peckered billy goat out here."

"God, I missed you," Livie smiled. "What's going on back home? I'm dying for news."

"Well, a dark cloud of controversy is hanging over the Silver Queen Corn Festival."

"Oh, Mama told me there might be a showdown looming. What happened?"

"The Town Council finally approved a request to ante up on the entertainment to draw a bigger crowd—you know, the Raleigh types. The problem is they didn't read the fine print on the $10,000 contract to know what band they really hired, a group called 'The Crotch Crickets.' They are most famous for a song about oral sex that got some air play in the 1980s. Outrage began ringing from all corners of the county with swiftness, and the fuddy-duddies on the Council had to go into closed session so that the county attorney could explain both the name of the band and the gist of the offending lyrics. The veterans are concerned that the uproar will detract from the patriotic spirit of the July Fourth holiday weekend, and the VFW has filed a formal petition with the city because they are sure attendance and thus the profits at their Brunswick stew fundraiser will be down. The PTA is hot because for the last three years, they've begged the Council for $10,000 to fund a county-wide third-grade field trip to the Outer Banks. The PTA presidents at each school sent home letters asking parents to boycott the festival and protect delicate ears from what was sure to be a musical orgy. And last but certainly not least, the whackadoodle street preacher with the megaphone on top of his holy roller conversion van has been circling the court house screaming about Sodom and Gomorrah. It's the most jacked up mess you've ever seen. I don't know what they're going to do."

"I do love me some rural controversy," Livie said with complete satisfaction. "The folks down here are nutty, just a very different variety of it. Listen, this is your vacation, so I didn't make any plans for you—other than dinner tonight with Luke at eight at Louie's Backyard."

"I hope he brings his 'A' game. At church on Sunday, your Mama slipped a fifty-dollar bill in my hand in exchange for pictures and a full report when I get back."

"Well, isn't that just like her. Did you keep the money?"

"Oh yeah, I'm on Team Mama Green for this one."

After spending the afternoon in the Mills Place pool like a pair of useless lumps, we walked down to Front Street and splurged on Lilly Pulitzer dresses to wear to dinner. On the trip back, we were treated to an astonishing Key West sun halo. I was convinced it was a sign from God calling me to stay an extra week.

We arrived at Louie's thirty minutes early to have a drink at the waterfront bar. She had no reason to be anxious, but the butterflies in Livie's tummy were crying out for a margarita.

The bay view that unfolded in front of us was unlike anything I'd ever seen. I sat there like a goober and filled up my phone storage capacity with picture after picture.

We could sense behind us that the air had just been sucked out of the room, and we turned around for a trouble check. He was wearing a white collared shirt, the top two buttons undone to reveal the *Atocha* coin on his broad chest. His tailored linen pants threw every woman in the room into a momentary swoon. He wore dark brown penny loafers with no socks and made his way through the maze of tables like he was on a runway. I froze with my margarita in midair, unable to break the paralysis.

"Ladies," he said when he reached the table.

Livie stood to collect a kiss.

"Luke, I'd like you to meet Blair Chrisman. Blair, this is Luke." Seeing that my struggle was legitimate and ongoing, Livie knew she'd have to carry things for a few more seconds. Turning back to Luke, she said, "Blair and I have been best friends for thirty years. If you didn't have a good sense of Avery, North Carolina, from hanging out with me, my Blair Bear will fill in the rest of the blanks for you."

"It's a pleasure to meet you, Blair. Judging by the way Livie laughs when she reads your texts, I think we're going to have a fun night together."

I'm pleased to report that I was able by that point to redeem myself and assume polite conversation. Luke delivered like he had been personally groomed by the best and the brightest of the Beaufort County NC Junior League. He asked thoughtful questions and listened intently to the answers. He was funny. He had table manners. He was a dream.

Before we left the table, I called for a toast: "To my very first Key West night. To the best fish tacos I've ever put in my mouth. To handsome locals. And to my dearest friend Livie, who will turn thirty-five next week. May this island deliver everything you've ever dreamed of."

*L*uke excused himself after dinner so we could have a girls night out in Old Town. Livie had rented a sassy little bike for me, and we launched out side by side into the night like we were ten-year-olds flying down Avery's Main Street again. Except this time, we were old enough to drink.

We did it all—Irish Kevin's, the Green Parrot, the Lazy Gecko, the Smokin' Tuna, Sloppy Joe's, Hog's Breath, and Captain Tony's before ending the night at the Wharf—where the bartenders poured for free and a mariachi band rattled the roof until two a.m.

Not exercising our better judgment, we decided to take a drunk bicycle tour of the island. Even in the still hours of the early morning, there were tourists out everywhere. We rode quietly for an hour—with the exception of a few near misses with parked cars that dissolved us both into pools of giggles.

By the grace of God, we made it safely back to the Truman Annex gates, the night security guard chuckling to himself about our questionable driving skills as we wobbled through the gates. As we made the turn down Emma Street a little bit after three a.m., the giant palm trees swished in the wind overhead.

"The rustling of those trees sounds like the pitter patter of the aboriginal rainstick," I said in my best Steve Irwin Crocodile Hunter voice, "an instrument that has been native to Australian music for hundreds of years." Then Livie started talking like the announcer in the Outback

Steakhouse commercials, inviting everyone trying to sleep in their million-dollar Truman Annex houses to "Come on in for shrimp on the barbie." I got so tickled that I lost control of my bike, ran up on the curb, and crashed (thankfully) on the fresh carpet of the manicured grass. It was just the funniest thing we'd ever gotten ourselves into.

Once we lugged our drunk behinds the rest of the way home, we collapsed into two beach chairs on Livie's porch.

"So, what's the damage back home?" Livie asked. "Have I been formally shunned in Avery yet?"

"Oh, hell no. The rumor mill did run wild there for a few weeks, but for the most part, it has calmed down. Tiffani Titless wasn't ready for it to stop, though. A few weeks ago after choir practice, I heard her spinning a yarn about you dancing on top of a bar down here."

"My God, that girl is mean as a striped snake. And that 'i' on the end of her name makes my skin crawl. You know, her creative storytelling keeps my Mama in a tizzy just about every day of the week."

"Don't worry. I've got your back. After the Wednesday night service, I put an anonymous note in the Prayer Warriors' 'Power of Prayer' request box."

"What did you do, Blair Bear?" Livie asked with mock consternation.

"It was just a minor crime, and I'm sure the Lord will overlook it considering how much trouble Tiffani causes. I just wrote that one of the many people from Avery on the cruise with her a few weeks ago was concerned for her soul. She had been observed walking into the Red Garter Saloon in Key West—the raunchiest full-nude strip club on the island, I was sure to point out. The sign outside that day said the place was hosting an amateur contest. I suggested that there may have been some video footage floating around on the Interwebs and that Preacher

Wayne might want to call her in for an intervention. And if she denied it, he might want to check her purse for excess one dollar bills."

"Please tell me you planted a big old roll of singles in her bag."

"Oh, no need. She keeps a wad of dollar bills on hand to make change for her Mary Kay customers—mostly blue hairs paying cash to buy one lipstick at a time."

"You are awful. And I love you for it."

"Here's the thing. In a small town, you might have two or three people rooting for you to fail when you take a chance like you did. But for every one of them, there are a hundred who are tickled by your initiative and are cheering for you on the sidelines. I'm really glad you came down here. I'll admit I was mighty worried at first, and this trip in large part was to make sure you were okay. I just needed to see with my own eyes that you were on the way to finding what you're after. You have no idea how good it feels to see you doing so much better than okay."

"I would have never taken that leap without knowing you'd be there to scrape me off the pavement with a spatula if necessary," Livie said.

"Well, I've always thought of myself as the wind beneath your wings."

"My bridge over troubled water."

"Lord, how many shots did we take?" I asked.

"Enough to remind me to start looking around for rest homes that will agree to let us live on the same hall together when the time comes."

Those last few mile markers before the Key West city limits can seem to the weary driver to take an eternity. Travelers in need of a place to wet their whistle can make a pit stop at the No Name Pub, located within the National Key Deer Refuge area. The bar, open since 1936, is a favorite of locals and tourists alike. Interestingly, the upstairs room once housed a brothel, which folded after a decade or so. The reason, legend has it, is that the fishermen were prettier than the girls.

9 don't know why it mattered to me so much, but I just had to see a Key deer before I flew out the next morning. Livie had been called into the Wharf to work an unscheduled afternoon shift, and she only refrained from telling Flit to shove it when Luke volunteered to drive me the thirty miles north to the habitat area, even though he'd seen Key deer hundreds of times and was exhausted from spending the day on the boat. It was about an hour before dusk when we arrived, and there wasn't a single deer to be found anywhere. Luke paraded between Mile Markers 29 and 33 for what seemed like forever without ever losing his patience or his interest in our conversation.

Finally, right around the time it got dark, I saw the tiniest little spotted head emerge from the brush behind the safety fence, looking hesitantly out toward the roadway. I squealed with delight through the open window of the truck like I had just seen Bigfoot. The poor animal probably crapped itself as it ran for its life back into the mangroves, and Luke ran two tires off the side of the road laughing about it all.

In that moment, my joy had little to do with a deer sighting. I knew my Livie had found the man who would humor her eccentricities, sacrifice for her happiness, and love her for the rest of her life.

"Oh, Livie." Mama's voice was shaking with excitement. "Blair told me all about Luke. She showed me the pictures, too. He's so handsome and tall. And I'm glad you haven't gotten mixed up with a short man. It's usually a mistake."

"I sure do like him, Mama, and I'm glad to know he's got the preliminary Avery seal of approval." Livie savored the moment because she really did love making her mother happy.

"Have you started cooking for him yet?"

"Yes, ma'am."

"Good. I'm going to mail you my recipe for chicken and dumplings in case you don't have it. Haven't met a man yet who could resist its power."

"Mama, I've also been volunteering as a tour guide at Hemingway's House, and I've offered a few guest lectures over there, too. Maybe you could tell the Prayer Warriors—possibly get my case status reduced from code orange to code yellow."

"Don't worry, baby—I'll tell them. In fact, I'll probably put this in the newsletter as a praise report. I'm on a roll. This will make two for me this week. Just the other day I led a telemarketer all the way in Delhi, India, to his salvation."

LIVIE

I need an impartial third party
to settle a bar dispute here. Think it through.
Emotions are running high. Was Keanu
Reeves hotter in "Speed" or "Point Break?"

BLAIR

Ooooh. Tough one. If we are
talking purely about Keanu
here, "Speed" wins. He was just
so attentive to Sandra Bullock's
needs. And that whole thing with
man-handling the bomb on the
bus was like sex on a stick. On
the flip side, an incredibly toned
Patrick Swayze with sun-kissed
hair raised the appeal of "Point
Break" as a whole, but that
wasn't Keanu's doing, per se.
Patrick's abs were a distraction
that could skew just about any
debate. "Speed" is my final
answer.

I'll deliver the verdict. Thanks for
sharing your insight and wisdom.

*L*ivie knew Mack would understand. She knew he wouldn't mind the two-thirty a.m. phone call and that he wouldn't ask any questions.

When she got to the side entrance on Olivia Street, the gate was unlocked. She pulled her bike through the opening in the fence to avoid drawing attention.

The ring of keys she was supposed to deposit in the planter on Mack's front porch later was waiting on the doorstep of the bookstore just as he promised.

It was a cool night clear of rain, but the sky flashed like a neon sign with pulses of harmless heat lightning, and the foliage whirled in the moderate wind.

In the darkness, she walked with bare feet through the damp grass, concentrating on the calming ripples of the water in the pool. She was grateful that Mack had turned off the pool lights; otherwise, the glory of the full moon hanging above would have been dulled.

Livie removed her tank top and shorts, standing there for a moment in her bra and underwear as she concentrated on the pace of her cleansing breaths. Then with no inhibition or second thought, she unhooked her bra and kicked off her panties, placing them on the head of one of the famous ceramic elephant seats around the pool deck.

The wind stirred again with extra force as her toes curled over the edge of the deep end. She could feel the goose bumps forming a trail up the small of her bare back.

Then she dove.

Ten or so rhythmic kicks propelled her underwater to the shallow end closest to the house. When she resurfaced, she pushed off the wall and returned to her point of entry in the deepest water—a good six feet over her head.

She stilled her mind to listen and slowed her movements to relax her heart rate, which had spiked with the stimulation of the colder-than-expected water.

Floating on her back with outstretched arms and wild Medusa hair swirling about her head, she realized the heavy moon was directly above her, its light casting a warm glow on the round of her belly and breasts as they protruded from the surface. One by one, Hemingway's cats gathered around the perimeter of the pool and observed like a cloud of witnesses.

She knew something was supposed to happen next, so she waited. Her ears were submerged, and all she could hear was the satisfying gurgle of moving water. The white noise allowed her to gain complete control over her breathing and to fully experience every sensory message being fired in her brain.

Out of nowhere came a spark of memory from one of the last classes she taught—about T.S. Eliot's 1922 poem "The Waste Land." Despite the blank stares from her students that rainy Monday morning, she had gotten uncharacteristically jacked up by the act of analyzing what was perhaps the most complicated and definitely the most important poem of the twentieth century. In the first four parts of the apocalyptic text, almost everything that could have gone wrong with the world has, and the people languish in their agony. The earth is dry and cracked from a lack of rain, the fields won't yield a harvest, and humankind is in ruins under the weight of a complete cultural collapse. Praying for rain, the people begin to hear the distant thunder in the culminating section.

Using the language of the Upanishads, Eliot crafted the universe's response to their pleas. The thunder rolled, and the people heard "DATTA," which means *to give*. The thunder rolled, and the people heard "DAYADHVAM," which means *to have compassion*. The thunder rolled, and the people heard "DAMYATA," which means *to have self-control*. The complexity of the poem's allusions and the density of hundreds of disorienting and confusing lines come to resolution with the repetition three times of a single promise: "Shantih shantih shantih"—*peace peace peace*. Though the poem ends before the cleansing rains come, the assurance that they are on the horizon pulls the people away from the brink of disaster. Their job is to follow the command: *give of yourself, have compassion, exercise self-control*.

Then Livie's command came in the stillness.

Let it fly.

She moved only enough to keep herself afloat and pondered the call.

Then she obeyed.

The exhausting drive to please everyone but herself.

The pressure to stoke her professional ambitions at the expense of her own well-being and serenity.

The fear of disappointing Mama and Daddy by choosing a path nobody else understood.

The worry that her unconventional choices would keep her from ever finding stability.

The guilt for doubting if God really knew what he was doing with her life.

The belief that Jimmy Buffett could somehow connect her to a part of herself that she couldn't access on her own.

She let it fly. And Ernest Hemingway's swimming pool water washed it all away.

On the morning of her thirty-fifth birthday, Livie awoke very early to ride her bike out to Stock Island. It was a six-mile cycle to the Lobster Yard, but she wanted to begin the next year of her life the right way. She pulled up to his place less stinky and sweaty than she thought she would be just as she knew he would be stirring around the docks. Archipelago was supervising as Luke loaded the empty plastic bushels he would need in case the shrimp were hopping that morning. He hadn't bothered to put on a shirt yet, and Livie sang the Lord's praises for it.

"Archie, go give the birthday girl some slobber," Luke said when he noticed her walking down the sidewalk.

The pup complied, trotting over to Livie and collapsing at her feet like he had lost the will to go on. The sweet little thing just wanted to be a blessing.

Her only birthday wish then came true: She lost herself in the comfort of Luke's steady arms, burying her face in the sweet aroma of his chest.

"I'm glad you're here," he said softly. "I wasn't sure I'd see you today to give you your gift."

Livie reluctantly released her grip so he could walk inside. A few seconds later he came out with a small parcel he'd wrapped in the brown wax paper and twine he used to package smaller orders of shrimp for individual customers.

"I hope I got the right one," he said with a shy smile.

Livie slowly untied the twine and folded back the thick paper. Then she didn't breathe for a few seconds.

First she saw the black block letters on the blue background announcing the author: HEMINGWAY. Then she recognized the iconic illustration of the humble Cuban fishing village beside the ocean.

It was a first edition of *The Old Man and the Sea.*

She didn't know how her face should handle the disbelief. *He remembered, and he went to a lot of trouble and expense to find a first edition.*

Nervously, she opened the cover to check the pages and convince herself that it was all real. And there it was on the title page: Ernest Hemingway's distinctive autograph.

"Your birthday was celebrated in grand style at Avery First Baptist Church this morning," I said.

"What are you talking about?" Livie asked with great trepidation.

"In between the welcome for new visitors and the offertory, Preacher Wayne used the big screen normally reserved for his sermon notes to project a humongous picture of you and Luke at Louie's that night. He wanted everyone in the congregation to know that Dr. Olivia Green, 'who just celebrated her birthday, is doing very well in Key West, Florida, with her new job as a scholar in residence at Hemingway's House and with her new boyfriend, who Sister Green is confident will be a member of the family sooner rather than later.'"

"I'm afraid to ask, but what was the reaction?"

"Well, your brother nearly fell out of his chair he was laughing so hard. Your Daddy put his elbows down on his knees and his face in his hands. Mama, on the other hand, beamed like the Ocracoke Lighthouse and accepted the chorus of 'Hallelujahs,' the likes of which have never been heard in that sanctuary, even counting that time it was announced that the little girl with the gimp foot in Greenville we'd been praying for was miraculously healed. And I know exactly what set the whole thing in motion. Right before Sunday School, I saw your Mama walking into Preacher Wayne's office with a covered dish, and I'm willing to wager my right kidney that your Mamaw's frosted brownies were in there."

"You know what?" Livie said after a long pause. "Good for her. Though not intentional, I've put her through the wringer this past year. So much of her happiness and pride comes through me—and Carter when he isn't acting a fool. We all know the cheese slid off her cracker a long time ago, but her love for us is just about the purest thing in the world. I hate that I missed seeing her smile. And maybe this will once and for all get me off the Prayer Warriors' watch list. Might even get my record expunged."

"That's certainly a possibility," I said, "especially after Coralynn Dellinger's infelicitous and very public fall from grace. Those old harpies have much bigger fish to fry now."

"Oh, not Coralynn. She's such a sweet potato. What happened?"

"Action 6 News was filming outside of the Sweet Dreams Motel on Route 24 for an expose about the increase in prostitution arrests there. Well, in the background shot as the reporter was interviewing Sherriff Tipton, Coralynn emerged from one of the rooms hand in hand with Marty Ballard."

"Marty 'BBQ' Ballard?" Livie interrupted.

"Yes, the very married Marty 'BBQ' Ballard, the same one who is running for the NC House. It was on the six o'clock news, and everybody was eating supper and watching when it aired."

"Well, let us gather at the River Jordan."

"And to make matters worse, Marty's opponent in the state race took the clip of the two lovebirds coming out of their nest and the 'Ladies of the Night' graphic from the Action 6 expose to create an ad that implies Marty had rented Coralynn for the evening. The campaign is paying to have the tacky thing run non-stop on all the channels. And a mailer with a screen shot of their exit emblazoned in red with the words 'REPENT ADULTERERS!'

landed in every mailbox in Avery. My guess is that the crazy street preacher was responsible for that part. There's a lot of mileage left in this one. It ain't going away."

"I should probably give Coralynn a call and see if she wants to come visit for a week and let this thing blow over. After all, we welcome wicked sinners with open arms down here."

Blue Marlin Jewelry

Mile Marker 81.5
81549 Old Highway
Islamorada, FL 33036
305-664-8004

BILL TO	INVOICE #	1978
Olivia Green	INVOICE DATE	06/26/0012

Invoice Total $856.00

DESCRIPTION		AMOUNT
Labor/Materials - 14 K gold pendant mount (Spanish 8 reales coin)		800.00
	Subtotal	800.00
	Sales TAX 7.0%	56.00

TERMS & CONDITIONS

PAID IN FULL

*L*ivie waited rather impatiently all morning for Luke to make his delivery at the Wharf. She was antsy to see if he noticed without her having to say anything.

Around nine thirty, her clock-watching paused with the entrance of a senior citizens line dancing club hungry for breakfast after their rehearsal. There wasn't nearly enough coffee ready to accommodate them all, so Livie ran back to the kitchen to get the largest urn filled and percolating. While she was back there, she mixed a bowl of batter for Hector, who was flipping pancakes as fast as his arms would go and singing the Desi Arnaz classic "El Cumbanchero" at the top of his lungs.

It was the perfect chance for Luke to wrap her in his arms from behind, pull her back into the kitchen pantry, and steal one of those kisses on her jawline just below her ear that sent her into orbit. He saw it hanging around her neck instantly, rested his chin on her shoulder, and offered a frisky "Hmmn" as he circled his finger on the coin suspended just above her breasts.

"There's no better place for that to hang than right there," he whispered low.

"I'm glad you like it," Livie said, satisfied with her surprise.

"'Like' isn't exactly the word. We'll talk about it when you get off. How many hours is that going to take?"

*M*ost locals suggest that Stock Island provides the last glimpse of what old Key West used to be. The town feels very much like a low-key cousin in Key West's increasingly high-profile family, which is probably why Mel Fisher decided to move to Stock Island's Key Haven neighborhood in the later years of his life. Of all the men and women who have traveled to the Keys to gamble on a roll of the dice, Mel's wager was perhaps the greatest of all. Everyone doubted him, but for sixteen years, he let it ride.

MURPHY GREEN
Hey, Dumpling. Question for you.
Do you know what a camel toe is?

LIVIE
Oh, Daddy.

Carter made a joke about it yesterday,
and I was too embarrassed to let
on that I didn't get it. I was going to
just look it up on the computer.
No. No. No. Don't do that. Oh,
God. It's when a woman wears
pants that are way too tight, and
you can see the outline of her
lady bits through the fabric.

That boy is such a freak.
Preaching to the choir, Daddy.

Okay then. That's all I've got.

*L*uke finally put his foot down. For a girl who ate shrimp with more enthusiasm than perhaps anyone he'd ever met, it was time that she earned her keep and learned how to catch them.

To ensure she didn't get the easy way out, Luke gave his mate a paid day off and subbed in Livie.

The morning started at five thirty a.m. in the engine room with delays. First, Livie supervised while Luke repaired a wiring problem that had become a perpetual issue on the *Anne Bonney*. Then Livie revealed that she had brought aboard contraband homemade cinnamon rolls with vanilla bourbon glaze. Then her residual excitement from seeing Luke fix a very powerful engine with his bare hands got the best of her, and they were waylaid below decks for a time.

They emerged into the sunlight an hour late for departure but in a fine mood. Livie unleashed the mooring lines, Luke lowered the outriggers, and they took to the open sea in time to witness the majesty of the sunrise.

Luke was a patient instructor, explaining not just what to do but why it should be done in terms that imbued even the mundane aspects of his job with meaning and dimension. She delighted in the poetry of the movements: *Prepare the doors, ready the nets, tie the bag lines, deploy, wait, winch in the nets, pop the bag lines, and repeat.*

Under the punishing tropical rays, they filled their bushels with the keepers while Livie learned which species in the bycatch to throw overboard. It was taxing and dirty work, but everything about it was marvelous.

LIVIE

Are you back from Kaeleigh Scronce's
wedding? I can't wait for the
postmortem wrap-up.

BLAIR

2:00 p.m. ceremony.
Outside. In August.

14 bridesmaids, each wearing a
different style of tulle ballgown in
an array of sherbet colors.

Two dogs as ringbearers, one of
which got in a coughing fit at the
altar while a very shaky soloist
coasted on fumes through "Ave
Maria."

No cake. Ice cream sundae bar
instead. Outside. In August.

Anal-retentive photographer.
Waited an hour and 45 minutes
for the bridal party to finish
with pictures and come to the
reception.

Black tie (even though the sun
was still up) yet they still served
those vile weenies in grape jelly.
I got to have a heat stroke in
my new cocktail dress while I
watched everybody eat those
nasty things. It was a very
special kind of hell.

Let's face it. Emily Post is dead,
and Martha Stewart did hard jail time.
We're a storm-bound ship without a
compass here. The best we can
do is hang on tight.

BROTHER
The Silver Queen Corn
Festival was a disappointment.

LIVIE
I've been waiting for an
eyewitness account.

The Crotch Crickets' performance
was picketed only by the street preacher,
his wife in a fundamentalist prairie dress,
and their 11 kids, all wearing earplugs
and holding "FORNICATORS WILL
BURN IN THE FIRE" signs.

Wait a minute. What were you
doing at a public fair/carnival? I
thought you vowed to never go
to another one.

I'll make an exception when
law enforcement have deemed
it an "extraordinary event" and
there's a decent chance I'll see
a clash between good and evil.

The docents who guide tours for thousands of tourists through Hemingway's Key West house each year answer the same questions, narrate the same script, and offer the same jokes day after day. They tell the tourists not to sit on the bed, not to cross the velvet ropes, not to touch the artwork, not to hold the cats, and not to pick the flowers.

In exchange, they get to experience the joy of the first-time visitor seeing the whole thing with fresh eyes. They catch a contact high from the men and women fulfilling their life-long dreams of peering through the iron gates into the great author's second-story writing studio, hoping some inspiration will float out of there and land on them. The docents realize the reward in transferring their passion for Hemingway's writing to a new generation of enthusiasts who will keep his legacy alive.

As far as Livie was concerned, she always came out ahead in the exchange at the end of each day.

*I*t definitely wasn't time to get up—that much she could tell by the color of the sky through the curtains of the bungalow's second-story window. It couldn't be any later than three a.m. The fact that she was awake had Archipelago and Don Ho concerned, and they wouldn't stop staring at her.

She inched out of bed trying to avoid disturbing the dynamic duo and thus awakening Luke. Then she grabbed her journal and pen off the nightstand on her way out to the balcony.

Once she was comfy in the hammock she and Luke loved to share on lazy weekends, she flipped to an empty sheet. The absolute stillness of the night created the wide open space she needed to process the swirl of thought that had interrupted her sleep. Without ceremony or any kind of fanfare, the well of her spirit began to flood with images of writers, musicians, poets, artists, paintings, sculptures, histories, theories, and connections she knew she was destined to explore. Her hand raced to follow her brainstorm as page after page was filled with ideas and then turned. She gave herself permission in the moment to sling open the door of that fragile place in her heart that it had been necessary to close off as she bolted away from the university years before. She felt it again as if it had never left—that tickle of wild curiosity that even a good scratch never seems to satisfy. She had made it happen. By putting her worries on a shelf to collect dust, she birthed an inconceivable and splendid dream into reality. And now, as she lay there on the porch in her pajamas as happy as she had ever been, she positively marinated in a glow of fresh excitement for the life that was to come.

Luke's alarm buzzed as the tiniest splash of pink began to dot the brushstrokes of the morning canvas. Livie rolled out of the hammock, savored a long stretch, and wondered where Mack Mason would be today. She needed to hug his neck.

The Thursday morning of Livie's last week at the Wharf in late June 2013 dawned bright and warm. It was a bittersweet crossroads, but one Livie was ready to embrace. A group of barely twenty-one-year-old raucous jocks had just bounded into the bar like the champions of the world, smoking cigars with the wrong ends cut and looking for a bathroom. Livie mixed rum punches for all of them to go, and as she poured the drinks into plastic cups, she was tempted to add straws and lids for the little guys. She had taught at a university long enough to know for certain that they were seniors on a lacrosse team, and she giggled with the satisfying realization that she would never have to grade any of their papers.

Of course, her final days as a waitress couldn't be easy. Blowing rains on Monday, Tuesday, and Wednesday had made every part of the job wretched and wet, with small crowds and laughable tips. The weather broke on Thursday, and the staff was optimistic. Unfortunately, everything in the Wharf seemed to break that day, too, including Hector's main freezer in the kitchen, both sinks in the women's restroom, and the electrical line to the main cooler behind the bar. The repairman had left twenty minutes before with the assurance that the cooler should be in good shape now. He'd be back in a few hours with the parts he needed to tackle the sinks and the freezer.

Livie got to spend the next half hour squatting over the disgusting floor behind the bar and restocking the cooler with citrus wedges and drink mixes. She was thinking about how badly the floor needed a mop and how badly she didn't want to be the one to do it. She didn't notice a new customer amble up to the bar in a straw hat, sunglasses, board shorts, and Bob Marley T-shirt.

When he spoke, it surprised her, but she registered the voice immediately. The distinctive Alabama drawl stopped her dead in her tracks.

"I hear the pancakes are pretty good. Could I please get a short stack with a side of grilled shrimp—as long as they're fresh?"

The night before, Mack had insisted that Jimmy stop by the Schooner Wharf for breakfast before he flew out, that there was an academic there posing as a waitress who needed to talk to him. Mack and Jimmy's reunions, though increasingly infrequent, always brought back happy memories of their very best times recording together in Nashville in Jimmy's country music days, especially the long studio hours working on the very first album, *Down to Earth*, before fame was even a thought. Jimmy was delighted to oblige his pal and even more delighted to spend the hour chatting with Livie Green Spottswood, the girl with an *Atocha* piece of eight around her neck, a wicked sense of humor, and one hell of a story to tell.

*I*t was folded up in the bottom of the Wharf's cash register drawer the whole time, but Livie knew it was meant to stay there. It wasn't intended for Jimmy Buffett—it was gifted to her as a talisman, one that ignited a restlessness in her spirit that she was unable to ignore.

When she clocked out for the last time on Friday, she left it there for the next traveler to find.

The ocean's alive with motion and magic
Let her wash out your props and you'll see
Your snarky and glum
Will be cured with the rum
In the shade of a swaying palm tree.
Don't worry, be happy, your barstool is waiting
At Kevin's or Tony's or Joe's
You live on an island
Where the sun's usually shining
And the highs wipe away all the lows.
The charter boat docks with the coolers quite empty
No tuna or wahoo to be found
With all that you spent
Hell, you won't make the rent
Maybe Captain will buy the first round.
Don't worry, be happy, your barstool is ready

At Kevin's or Tony's or Joe's
Your home is an island
Where the sun's usually shining
No hassles as you come and you go.
The sunset revival is staged every night
For the weary, the broken, the lost
It recharges their souls
And stokes their coals
Clears their credit with none of the cost.
Don't worry, be happy, your barstool is ready
At Kevin's or Tony's or Joe's
At least for today
Your job's far away
Let your whimsy decide where you go.
I refuse to wear shoes, they're a lame-ass attempt
To keep Caribbean souls in line
Find reason to fret
You deserve what you get
Climb aboard, bare feet are just fine.
Whatever your trouble, Key West has the answer
Whether you bring your worst or your best
Despite what you think
All you need is a drink
Let the island take care of the rest.

TWO LUCKY SHRIMP
FLOATING IN THE SEA
ANOTHER IN THE NET
FISHER MAKES THREE

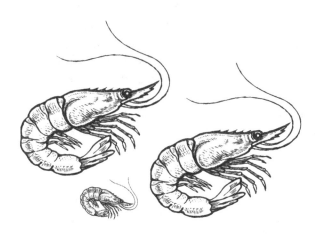

Toddling onto the porch of the bungalow with Archie at his feet and wearing only a pair of cowboy boots, a feathered pirate hat, and his big-boy underwear (which he'd just earned after showing potty training who was boss), three-year-old Fisher Maloney Spottswood waved his plastic cutlass at the imaginary buccaneers in pursuit of his treasure. After they moved to their new house on Emma Street in 2014 while Livie was pregnant, the first level of the bungalow had been converted into the office space the expanded fleet of Stock Island Shrimp Company vessels needed to meet the new demand in the Lower Keys for ethically sourced seafood. The bedroom upstairs had remained untouched, however, and it was the perfect place for a little tub of love to take an afternoon nap while his Mama worked through accounting spreadsheets or tinkered around with a new lecture for the next event at Hemingway's house.

Don Ho didn't especially care for Archie's incessant drool, but he was very fond of the idea of being in charge of an entire fishing village and supervising his very own dog, and for the past four years, he'd handled the responsibility with the utmost integrity and seriousness.

Since their "Little Fish" had come into the world, Mama and Daddy Green had become experts at "the FaceTime," conferencing themselves in multiple times a day. "The Beast" burned up the A1A about once a month when they just couldn't stand the distance anymore. They would just barely slow their roll and exit the motorhome like it was about to be engulfed in flames, showering Fisher in their hugs and kisses. When the grands were in town, Livie and Luke didn't see much of Fisher. He was either in the kitchen with Mimi, who was trying to find some way to sop up his sweetness with a biscuit, or somewhere on the road with Pops, moseying around the island in a wagon hitched to a bicycle.

*I*t was a Friday afternoon, and Livie had just heard the tell-tale sounds through the baby monitor that Fisher was awakening from a nap when a rumble of thunder shook the house. *DATTA, DAYADHVAM, DAMYATA,* she thought to herself, immediately recognizing the irony that she was probably the only person in the world laughing about a somber poem like *The Waste Land* in that moment. She picked up her sleepy, curly-headed baby and walked out to the dock, where they dangled their feet over the side, hoping for an appearance by their favorite local manatees. There were beautiful deep purple squalls out in the distance, and Livie breathed in the smell of the coming rain. Luke was always aware of storms on the water, and she knew she would see the profiles of his trawlers appear one by one on the horizon soon. She and Fish would be there to help offload the catch—some of it purposefully stored at sea in light loads by the captain so that his boy could carry them into the new ice house next to the bungalow.

Uncle Mack was coming to dinner on Emma Street that night for a party to celebrate his first fat royalty check. It turns out there were anxiety-ridden men and women all over America who just needed to color. Livie was hoping Luke would bring back something tasty she could throw into a gumbo pot to feed a crowd. Their honeymoon in New Orleans had encouraged her to learn how to cook like a cajun. She and Fish would twirl around the kitchen dancing to zydeco music while she experimented with jambalayas and étouffées with varying degrees of intensity. Luke was completely in favor of her trial and error and willingly offered his taste-testing skills whenever necessary.

It was in quiet moments like this—with Fisher distracted by the arrival of the manatees—that inspiration usually hit her. She had long ago learned the reflections that seemed like fleeting, meaningless thoughts were really God's way of talking to her, sometimes to affirm her choices, sometimes to comfort her in the sting of a decision that caused a detour.

Just as she saw the profile of the outriggers underneath the weighty cloud line, one of those thoughts was gifted to her:

If you can somehow manage to find a way to end your day on a dock—with sun-quenched toes suspended over crystal blue water—you'll be as much ahead in the rat race as you'll ever need to be.

She wrapped her arms around her precious nugget, who was chirping with delight at the antics of the manatees surfacing for air.

"Let's do the shrimp song again, Mama," he begged, his sweet little face just inches from hers. He held up his chubby fingers and counted with the verses:

> One little shrimp
> Lonely and blue
> Another in the net
> Shrimp makes two
> Two lucky shrimp
> Floating in the sea
> Another in the net

Fisher makes three
Three silly shrimp
Happy as can be
Love is enough
For you and for me

"So, I did a thing," I said over the phone.

"You better not have gone to Pamplona to run with the bulls without me," Livie blurted out with surprising ferocity.

"No, we promised we'd save that for our fortieth year," I said. "I'm good to my word."

"Well spill, Bill."

"So, Tad Triplett came into Dr. Schwalm's office late yesterday afternoon for a yearly physical and some blood work to manage his cholesterol. When he was getting up on the exam table, the back side of his gown popped open, and what I saw made me think of him in quite a new way."

"You do remember he's Tiffani's older brother, right?" Livie asked. "The one who has stalked us like a banshee for nearly four decades?"

"We'll get to that part in a minute," I assured her. "So, later on my stomach started growling while I was drawing his blood, and before long, his belly started rumbling, and we both got a good chuckle out of it. When I brought in his discharge paperwork and was about to send him on his way, he asked if I'd like to ride over to Hickory Grove with him to eat at the Cracker Barrel seeing as how we were both so hungry. And I did have a hankering for pinto beans and cornbread."

"Blair, Blair, Blair."

"So after we ate, we sat at the table for another hour talking. He is ridiculously funny. And cute. And very single. How did we not notice it?"

"Oh, I've always thought he was adorable. It's just that the idea of being Tiffani's sister-in-law was enough to make me want to pull all the skin off my face."

"Well, we weren't ready to come back to town yet, so we stopped at the Superette and got a case of Coors Light and rode out to the old drive-in."

"I thought they closed it a few years ago."

"They did, but you can still get in there. We made most of the case disappear …."

"Oh God."

"… And then I rode him like a racehorse in the Kentucky Derby right there in the back of his Mustang."

"Stop it. Stop it. Stop. It."

"I did it, Livie Lu, and I'm probably going to do it again tonight. And maybe even tomorrow. He's a peach. And a good sport in the sack."

"Tiffani Triplett is going to find a way to make sure you burn in a special part of hell for this."

"She'll try hard, and the idea of it adds an extra layer of joy to all of this for me."

BROTHER
Any chance I can squat in
your guest room next week?

LIVIE
Yay! Of course.
What's the occasion?

Mack asked if I wanted to
come down again and back him
up on a week of gigs playing
percussion – tambourine, cowbell,
maracas. He's booked two
bars a day this time.

And I miss the Fish. He's growing
up too fast. I'm going to blink,
and he'll have a fake I.D.

He's going to blow his top when I
tell him Uncle C is coming again.
But you have to behave this
time. Luke and I just got him
to stop saying, "Hey Mama" to
every woman he sees.

*T*he worn brakes of the tourist trolley groaned to a stop in front of the Mile Marker 0 sign on Whitehead Street while the megaphoned guide spewed historical trivia at an auctioneer's pace. The bus was full of knobs easily identifiable by their matching ON/OFF trolley stickers and their blistered sunburns as they lined up for their predictable dose of safe, spoon-fed vacation experience. A sullen couple from Cleveland at the rear of the trolley had long ago given up on trying to piece together the mish-mash of the guide's rapid-fire narration. "I don't get it," Bob said. "We are at mile 0, but the road keeps going down that way. I thought the sign marked the end. This is quite a disappointment, Phyllis. And this place is so bloody hot. It's eight forty-five in the morning, and I already need another bath."

"Maybe at the next stop we can get off and go back to get one of those drinks in the coconut shells with the little umbrellas," Phyllis said, her feigned attempt at a positive attitude falling flat. "Or we could go back to the ship early. Nothing says we have to stay on the island the whole three hours."

*E*very night after dinner, Luke, Livie, and Fisher took advantage of the tourists being corralled for an hour at the Sunset Festival and walked the entire distance of Whitehead Street—past the Southernmost Point, Hemingway's house, the Green Parrot, the site of Livie's absurd car wreck, and Mile Marker 0.

Hitting those marks every night always made Livie reflect on her unimaginable journey. On this night in early November 2017, the sign with the big zero had special significance, as it had been almost exactly six years ago that Luke walked into the Wharf with that beautiful crate of shrimp.

"I've been thinking," she said after walking eight or nine blocks in silence. Fisher had just found another palm tree acorn on the sidewalk—a running game they played each night—and he was preoccupied with putting the prize in his bag and counting the number he'd already found. "For the vast majority of people, zero is a beginning point, the place to start the trip toward something better. We work ourselves into a froth so that our zero balance gets back in the black. We scramble for points to take our team past the goose egg on the scoreboard. The negative connotation of zero as the absence of a necessary thing is turned on its head (as are most things) in the Keys. Here, in a place where life is measured out in mile markers, zero is the grand finale—the destination for the pilgrimage of the wandering soul instead of the starting block."

"I've lived here all my life, and I've never given that silly sign much of a thought," Luke said, gathering three acorns from a flower bed and leaning down to offer Fisher a high five. "Your wheels never stop spinning, do they?"

"It's a funny thing, really," Livie said as they crossed through the Truman Annex gates and entered the cocoon of their idyllic little neighborhood. "And here we are living right around the corner from it."

WORKS CITED
AND CONSULTED

Allman Brothers. *Eat a Peach*, Capricorn, 1972.
   Idlewild South, Capricorn, 1970.
Baker, Carlos, Ed. *Ernest Hemingway: Selected Letters*
   1917-1961. New York: Scribner's 1979. Print.
Brooks, Randy. *Grandma Got Run Over by a Reindeer*,
   Elmo 'n' Patsy, 1979.
Bruce, Ed. "Mammas Don't Let Your Babies Grow Up
   To Be Cowboys." *Ed Bruce*, United Artists, 1975.
Buffett, Jimmy. *A1A*, Dunhill, 1974.
   Banana Wind, Margaritaville/MCA, 1996.
   Barometer Soup, Margaritaville /MCA, 1995.
   Changes in Latitudes, Changes in Attitudes, ABC,
     1977.
   Coconut Telegraph, MCA, 1981.
   Down to Earth, Barnaby, 1970.
   Floridays, MCA, 1986.
   Fruitcakes, Margaritaville/MCA, 1994.
   Havana Daydreamin', MCA, 1987.
   High Cumberland Jubilee, Barnaby, 1976.
   Hot Water, MCA, 1988.
   Last Mango in Paris, MCA 1985.
   Living & Dying in ¾ Time, ABC, 1974.
   Off to See the Lizard, MCA 1989.

One Particular Harbor, MCA, 1983.

A Pirate Looks at Fifty. New York: Ballantine, 2000.
  Print.

Riddles in the Sand, MCA, 1984.

A Salty Piece of Land. New York: Back Bay Books,
  2005. Print.

Somewhere Over China, MCA, 1982.

Son of a Son of a Sailor, ABC, 1978.

Tales from Margaritaville. New York: Mariner Books,
  2002. Print.

Volcano, MCA, 1979.

Where is Joe Merchant? New York: Mariner Books,
  2003. Print.

A White Sport Coat and a Pink Crustacean,
  ABC, 1973.

You Had to Be There, ABC, 1978.

Carlisle, Rodney, and Loretta. *Key West in History: A
  Guide to More Than 50 Sites in Historical Context*.
  Sarasota: Pineapple Press, 2015.

Cook, Jeff, Teddy Gentry, Mark Herndon and Randy
  Owen. *Christmas in Dixie*, RCA, 1982.

The Crocodile Hunter, starring Steve Irwin, Animal
  Planet, 1996-2007.

Eliot, T. S. "Tradition and the Individual Talent."
  The Norton Anthology of Theory and Criticism. Ed.
  Vincent B. Leitch. New York and London: W.W.
  Norton & Company, 2001. Print. 1092-1098.

Frost, Robert. "Birches." *Robert Frost: Selected Early
  Poems*. Claremont: Coyote Canyon Press, 2009.
  Print.

Hemingway, Ernest. *The Old Man and the Sea*. New York:
  Scribner, 1994. Print.

The Sun Also Rises. New York: Scribner, 2006. Print.

To Have and Have Not. New York: Scribner, 1993.
Print.

Jackson, Michael. "Billie Jean." *Thriller*, Epic, 1983.

Lyon, Eugene. *The Search for the Atocha*. Port Salerno:
Florida Classics, 1989. Print.

Maloney, Walter C. *Sketch of the History of Key West,
Florida*. Gainesville: University of Florida Press,
1968. Print.

Marley, Bob. "No Woman, No Cry." *Natty Dread*, Island,
1975.

Moore, Marianne. "Poetry." *The Norton Anthology of
Modern Poetry*. Eds Richard Ellmann and Robert
O'Clair. New York: W.W. Norton & Company,
1973. Print.

"No Name Pub." Web. 9 June 2017.

Oliver, Charles M. *Ernest Hemingway A to Z: The
Essential Reference to the Life and Work*. New York:
Checkmark, 1999. Print.

Pound, Ezra. *The Cantos*. New York: New Directions,
1996. Print.

Quist, Karen. "Historic Tavernier Hotel Reopens."
Florida Keys News. 13 August 2010. Web. 1 June
2017.

Rountree, Bob, and Bonnie Gross. "Road Trip: Florida
Keys Mile-Marker Guide." *FloridaRambler.com*. 25
May 2017. Web. 2 June 2017.

Simmons, Richard. "Sweatin' to the Oldies."

Simon, Paul. "Me and Julio Down by the Schoolyard."
Paul Simon, Columbia, 1972.

Smith, Jedwin. *Fatal Treasure: Greed and Death, Emeralds
and Gold, and the Obsessive Search for the Legendary
Ghost Galleon Atocha*. Hoboken: John Wiley &
Sons, 2003. Print.

"Spottswood Companies." *Spottswood.com*. 2009. Web. 25 May 2017.

Stevens, Wallace. *Collected Poems*. New York: Alfred A. Knopf, 1990. Print.

The African Queen. Dir. John Huston. Horizon Pictures, 1951. Film.

Thelma & Louise. Dir. Ridley Scott. Metro-Goldwyn-Mayer, 1991. Film.

Von Harten, H.H., Jr. *Little Geech: A Shrimper's Story*. Hilton Head: Lydia Inglett, 2011. Print.

Wilkinson, Jerry. "The Florida Keys Memorial." *KeysHistory.org*. Web. 6 June 2017.

"History of Key West." *KeysHistory.org*. Web. 8 June 2017.

"History of Stock Island." *KeysHistory.org*. Web. 9 June 2017.

ACKNOWLEDGEMENTS

Special thanks are due to:

Grant Roland and **Megan McDowell** in Investor Relations at Mel Fisher's Treasures in Key West, for providing wonderful insights about the Division Week festivities.

Dr. Marissa Schwalm, for offering peer response to early drafts that turned out to be spot-on. This book is better because you critiqued it. You are the best colleague I could ever hope to have.

Dustin Fryar, a real-life groundskeeper at the Ernest Hemingway Home and Museum in Key West. Our quick conversation in May 2017 may not have seemed like much, but it had a profound impact on several scenes in the book. Thanks for taking the time to answer my nosey questions.

My aunt, **Fredda McDonald,** for loaning me the Saint Simons Island cottage for several writing retreats that were instrumental in the crafting of this story. I am incredibly grateful.

Pat and **Kristy Williams,** for providing loads of inspiration on our first trip to the island together. Here's to many more adventures to come.

Beverly Rhyne Bruce, for offering a free (hypothetical) jewelry setting appraisal.

Brandon Besecker, for sharing his knowledge of shrimping. When I grow up, I want to have your salt life.

Courtney Smith and **Lauren Tipton,** my two muses for the Blair character. You are both crazier than a bunch of loons, and I'll love you until the end of time for it.

And last but certainly not least, **Chris** and **Miller Oliphant.** My happy life with you made it possible to write such a happy story—no imagination necessary.

ABOUT THE AUTHOR

Dr. Ashley Oliphant is an associate professor of English and the chair of Humanities at Pfeiffer University. Her teaching specialties include twentieth-century American literature, literary modernism, and rhetoric and composition. Unlike the main character of this book, she is not dissatisfied with her job and at risk for flight. In fact, learning in the classroom alongside her students is one of her greatest joys.

She is the author of three other books: *Shark Tooth Hunting on the Carolina Coast*, *Hemingway and Bimini: The Birth of Sport Fishing at "The End of the World,"* and a dissertation titled *Hemingway's Mixed Drinks: An Examination of the Varied Representation of Alcohol Across the Author's Canon.* She is a longtime member of the Hemingway Society and a contributor to *The Hemingway Review.*

Additionally, she is an animal welfare advocate in her local community. She is dedicated to ending the use of gas chambers to euthanize animals and to educating citizens and elected officials about the merits of the No Kill Philosophy. Her county shelter is striving to be the first No Kill municipal facility in the state of North Carolina.

In her spare time, Oliphant likes to float in her swimming pool with her husband and son, play the ukulele in her hammock, and wait for the next trip to Key West to roll around. Her lifelong dreams are to own a signed first edition of Hemingway's *The Old Man and the Sea* and to meet Jimmy Buffett.

.

CPSIA information can be obtained
at www.ICGtesting.com
Printed in the USA
JSHW021433020323
38379JS00002B/148